FAITH
RIVENS

Eléonore

an
INÍONAOFA
novella

<u>**Dedication**</u>

To my Nana and Papa,

You gave me the gift of unconditional love and the confidence to try.

To my Mommy and Daddy,

You gave me the gift of my passion for stories and the courage to pursue my dreams.

To my sister,

You gave me the gift of a kindred spirit and a forever friend to walk this life with.

CHAPTER ONE

A Hunter

From the Journal of Étienne Dormant
Why do we hunt demons?
Because we inherited the duty from those that came before us.
Because the world we know will cease to exist if we do not.
Because it's a lot more fun than sitting behind a desk and counting numbers.

- November 1st 1993

There were demons to kill, but first I needed a cup of coffee.

The nearest café offered a variety of frappés, lattés, and mochas, but all I needed was a good strong, dark roast black from Canada's oldest coffee shop. An extra three blocks of walking was worth the bitter brew that steeled my nerves and jolted my brain. One sip was enough to get the juices flowing. Three more and I could feel the anticipation building. Ready and willing to slit some throats.

It was a little after nine o'clock in the evening and the night life of Downtown Montreal was quickening. Saint Catherine Street was a crowded hub of the young and yearning. Clubs, bars, pubs: those were the places that called their name. I couldn't hear what the revellers did; the only voice in my range beckoned me to the open area of Dominion Square.

It was a rowdier crowd that gathered there. Druggies and drunks. The putrid stench had my nose wrinkling and eyes rolling. At least the demons I fought were physical.

Eyes surveyed me as I went. Maybe it was the short red hair that caught their attention; it definitely wasn't the hazel brown eyes. I didn't have the Marilyn bombshell body that would turn heads either. It could have been the long brown coat that I wore over my burgundy dress, grey leggings, and tall black boots.

Or maybe I was just being paranoid and over-observant. It could sometimes be a side effect of the job, and tonight I was especially on edge.

Most nights, I stalked the streets trying to detect evil with what some would call a sixth sense. Tonight, however, Sinéad had warned me that something bad was going to go down. It was rare for her to give me a missive, preferring to offer only spiritual aid, so chances were high that something significant would take place this evening. The thought of a big brawl was exhilarating.

Leaning against a tree, I took a moment to give the park a once over.

Among the derelicts that fumbled along the path in rings of smoke, small families and couples meandered. They placed large enough distances between themselves and the unwanted as if the space could protect them from the sins, that through downcast gazes, they could pretend that the unfortunates weren't there at all. It was lies. Some of them realized it; others were blind enough to believe they were doing the best by it.

Then there was the girl. She was a slender figure dressed in what one might call professional attire: a grey pencil skirt, a tucked in white blouse that clung to what little curves she had without emphasising them. She did not avert her eyes as the others did. She met the stares of the inebriated and high. And they met hers right back. They clung to her regard with such desperate need and, just like that, I knew that she was the one I had been waiting for.

I appraised her again. She looked to be three or four years my junior, just in the cusp of her twenties, with hazel locks shorn just shy of her shoulders. She wore glasses, thin navy frames that sat atop her nose. Behind them, greyish-green eyes twinkled with kindness. She strolled leisurely, the smile on her face one of compassion and promise. A stereotype of the goodly woman. She was my demon.

That really was my sixth sense talking. Demons gave off a scent that most people couldn't smell. I could, though, just like dogs could hear shrill whistles.

She was my big bad, but what was her big bad plan?

The worst thing I could imagine her doing was shedding her disguise entirely to reveal her true form and setting fire to the whole square. But she wouldn't do that.

Would she?

The girl stalked towards a particularly rowdy group of young men smoking joints in the shadow of the trees near the east side of the square. Behind them loomed the Sunlife Building, an edifice whose architecture drew parallel to Grecian structures, with its towering pillars and white marble facade.

I kept my distance from her, settling on a bench that gave me a perfect view of her movements, close enough to hear what she was saying without drawing her suspicion. My hand fell underneath my trench coat to where my father's dagger was safely stashed in a hideaway pocket sewn into the lining. I took hold of the hilt and waited. Knowing that Trudeau—my father's name for the dagger— was there eased my desire to just kill her already.

I would let things play out a bit, see where they went, then make my move.

"T'en une fag?" A lean boy with shaggy black hair that covered most of his dirty face leaned towards her, his eyes dimmed by the drugs he poisoned his body with.

She shook her head. "I have something to offer you."

"Ah, oui?"

"Oui." She nodded and reached into the satchel worn around her shoulder.

I rose, my senses tingling, not unlike the way Peter Parker's might have at the sight of the Green Goblin. Though she was more of a spider than I was.

From the bag emerged a vial of purple liquid.

"You will enjoy this more, I think." She dangled the bottle before them, a tempting gift that the lot of them ogled with hazy, craving gazes.

"What eez eet?" The shortest one asked.

"Something that will take away your pain. It will make you strong. It will make you invincible."

"Combien?" The lanky one enquired.

The girl laughed. "We can determine a price at a later date."

I had heard enough. She was one of those bargaining demons, selling wares to humans in exchange for their souls. Whatever was in that bottle was nothing good. The boys had a better chance of surviving the next ten years sticking to their habit of getting high.

I moved in.

The girl turned only as one of the lad's eyes shifted to where I stood.

"Ah," she murmured, the vial slipping back into her bag. "Huntress."

My brows descended over my eyes. "Bitch."

She tittered, her middle finger rising to balance her glasses over her nose once again. "Will you exorcise me here?"

"I don't like an audience."

"I won't go quietly."

"I wasn't expecting you to."

"What ze fuck eez going on?"

The boys were still watching us, their clouded stares now utterly bewildered.

"Vous devez partir. Go!" I shooed them away.

Dumbfounded creatures, they didn't move.

"What now, Huntress?"

At best, I had three options open to me. First, to slit her throat and set her body aflame—hopefully, her flesh would be reduced to ashes before the police and firemen came bearing down on the place. Second, confiscate her satchel, part ways as mutual enemies and carefully stalk her to a more remote location where I could end her life without any witnesses. Third, let whatever evil things were going to happen, happen and deal with the repercussions later.

"Give me your bag."

"If you want a taste, all you have to do is ask."

The addicts were lumbering away, at last, disinterested by our back and forth banter. She took note of their departure with a scowl.

"You've chased away my clientele," she whined.

"No point holding onto that then." I gestured towards her bag. "Let me take it into custody, and you can walk away. Alive."

Her eyes appraised me dubiously. Then, with a shrug, her satchel slipped off her shoulder. She kept a hand on it. "I'm doing this in good faith."

"You have plenty of that." I kept my tone dry. It would be better if she thought I was taking this as seriously as a stain on a t-shirt.

The bag fell into my waiting hands. I restrained the urge to look through its contents, nonchalantly sliding it over my shoulder.

"Hopefully, the next time we meet will be under better circumstances."

It will definitely be better for me. "Just don't let me catch you around here anymore."

"Promise." She held ten uncrossed fingers up, then turned on her heel and strode away at a leisurely pace.

While she sauntered off, I turned a full three-sixty to assure myself that there were no other threats. There weren't at the moment, but that didn't mean they wouldn't come. Waiting around to see if anything else happened was one option, but the demonic dealer could not be allowed to wander off. If I weren't alone in this, I wouldn't have to worry about it. I preferred working alone anyway.

There had been a time when I had protected these streets with my father. His death almost ten years past had changed all that. It had changed a lot.

There was no time to linger in memories or panic over the choice I had to make. There were three options before me. One, stick around and see if anything else happened. Two, follow the demon and hope that I wasn't abandoning the square to some kind of apocalypse. And three, go home and sleep and pretend like demons didn't exist.

I stalked the demon southwards, towards Réné-Levesque Street and the Mary Queen of the World Cathedral. The white dome stood stark against the dark canvas of night. The last time I had chased one of her kind into it, it had been a good lesson in the strength of the 'sacred sanctuary' stories I'd heard. Invisible demonic figure repelling force field. That's what I would call it.

She turned east onto Réné-Levesque and kept straight on it for ten blocks. I trailed her, keeping a good distance between us. She melted easily into the crowd and I lost track of her more times than I cared for. Anxiety rose in my stomach, but then I caught wind of her again and adrenaline would ease the rushing unease. My head was starting to ache, as it often did when I was under this kind of stress. Unfortunately, I had left my painkillers at home, which meant seven hours relief would have to wait until after the vanquishing.

Finally, she turned up a quieter road. Darker too. A street lamp flickered ominously, perhaps a little too on point. I half expected a flash of lighting, but real life was never like the movies.

She faltered and I leaped into the nearest doorway, careful to avoid any chance of being seen. Trudeau was out now, clutched to my chest, expectant. Had she caught sight of me? Was I going to emerge from the threshold and find her looming there in all her demonic glory?

I chanced a glance after five more breaths, just in time to catch sight of her slipping into an apartment building.

"Merde!" I cursed and darted forward as the door shut behind her. I tried the knob, but it wouldn't budge.

I fumbled quickly through my pockets for the Swiss Army knife my dad had left me—it didn't have a name, but I liked to call it useful. I brought out the lock pick he had fashioned: 'the universal house key' he had termed it. I brought it into the lock and shifted it once then twice before a click resounded.

Triumphant, I strode in, ready for the fight that would have to end with her demise. A staircase greeted me, one that led up to another door. It was a dark passageway, but I could tell that it was narrow and tall. Was she waiting for me somewhere in the shadows? Or was she already undressing in her room, assured of safety for the night? I was really hoping for that last one.

With Trudeau still clutched in my grip, I ascended, taking care but not taking my time. I assumed that this was her place, but there was every chance that a human lived here. I couldn't hesitate in case she was threatening an innocent life.

The door at the top proved to be unlocked when I turned the brass knob.

That should have been my first warning.

The hall that I stepped into was dimly lit by a single lamp on a wood table. The walls, a dark grey, were covered in black runes. Spells.

"Ah, damn," I muttered, realizing then that I had never been the predator.

Like a stupid fly, I had fallen into the spider's trap.

CHAPTER TWO

A Trap

An evil as old as the dawning of the earth, demons exist on a plane that is not our own. The Ancients of older days found that they could reach into that world and bring those apparitions into the reality of our age. Over time, the barriers between our worlds weakened and cracks appeared between the two, allowing demons to seep through. Demons summoned by sorcerers are bound to their word. Its the ones that creep over on their own accord that you have to watch out for.

- April 4th 1994

I would have cursed myself for my foolishness, but I couldn't risk dividing my attention. Survive first, then self-reproach.

Trudeau was still in my grasp, and now it was joined by a rapier that I had bought off a medieval vendor six years prior. He hadn't realized that the slender blade was coated with a faint layer of crystallised holy water, crafted especially for demon destruction. He had sold it to me for a hundred dollars. I had named her Éponine.

I hoped to call her bloody before the night was over.

I revolved on the spot as the floorboard creaked behind me. The demonic woman was there, but she was no longer a woman, now she was a full demon. Her form, shadowy and wispy, revealed that she was only newly summoned. A blue creature with purplish hues, her eyes were a cool yellow, her nose hooked like a beak. Horns on her head curved back then forth, and fangs glistened when she smiled at my surprise. She was a tall and lean thing that almost towered over me. The sight of her was enough to frighten me. What really got to me was the fact that she wasn't alone.

A sorcerer—her master, no doubt—stood a little behind her, dressed in plain clothes, dark jeans and a loose fitting navy blue shirt. His brown hair was coiffed, his green eyes twinkled mischievously. He was the kind of guy I would have done a double take on if I'd passed him on the street.

"Mademoiselle Dormant."

He knew my name.

What hellhole of trouble had I stumbled into this time?

"There's no need for those." The sorcerer gestured at my blades with a tilt of his head.

Éponine raised a little higher, Trudeau stuck out threateningly. "Guess Lassie's going to get a nice bone for fetching this stick, huh?"

Lassie didn't even flinch; I guess she hadn't been introduced to pop culture yet. Shame that she wouldn't ever get the chance.

The sorcerer's lips curved, amused. "Amaranth is a faithful companion."

Amaranth purred contentedly.

I knew enough about sorcerers and the demons they summoned to know that some enjoyed more intimate relationships. The image popped into my mind before I could stop it.

"So, Eléonore, will you be coming quietly?"

"If I had known we were going on an adventure, I would have packed my bags."

"I assure you that won't—"

I leaped forward, preferring to cut the conversation short. These words were boring and my head was really beginning to pound. Before anyone could move, Éponine sliced Amaranth from head to toe.

9

A piercing scream fled her lips, and she flamed out of existence, leaving a pile of ash. I was lucky that she was only a few months old. A more mature demon would still be standing.

I pointed my blade at her sorcerer next, only hesitating in my kill because he was about to become a resource of information. "How do you know my name?"

"That was unnecessary."

"Where were you planning on taking me?" I tried a different angle, but I had little hope of getting anything else from him.

"Amaranth was merely serving me."

"And who do you serve?"

The sorcerer laughed then, not a cackle, just a booming, rich sound of true amusement. "Myself, largely."

A surge of magic billowed from his dangling hand. I sensed it before the first flicker of light sparked between his fingers.

Trudeau cut his throat before he could attack, slicing through his jugular. He dropped to the floor.

I shouldn't have killed him. It was a rookie mistake I knew better than to make. But I was exhausted and frustrated. He had sent out a demon to lure me to this place. He had sought me out specifically. Someone knew my name. And if they knew that—

I dashed across the town, bloodstained and furious. Adrenaline had kicked in full force and I was ready to run a 5k. Which was a good thing, because my apartment was just about half that distance from the sorcerer's hideout. People stared, but no one interfered. Kitty Genovese should have been a warning against bystander apathy, but people have short memories. You would think that a woman dying in an apartment because neighbours were too lazy to respond to her screams would have compelled people to be more alert.

At least weaving through the crowd of late night revellers made it difficult for one to stalk or be stalked. I was worried that someone had found where I lived, but I wasn't about to make the mistake of leading someone there on the off-chance that they hadn't.

I covered the area in under thirty minutes. It wouldn't have taken even half that long if not for the fact that the streets were bustling. I had done my share of roof hopping in the past, but I couldn't imagine leaping through the air tonight. I was grounded by the weight of a panicked heart.

The small condo that I called home was on the third floor of a complex. It wasn't the cheapest thing in Montreal, nor was it the cream of the crop either. It made do for the purposes it had to serve—not that there were many.

Provide shelter: Check.

Close to work: Check for day. Check for night.

Remain outside the radar of possible demonic enemies...

Before this night, I had been confident enough in that last proviso too.

I took the steps, two at a time, undaunted by the challenge.

My heart race accelerated the closer I drew to my destination, the closer I came to discovering if Étienne was safe.

The door to our apartment was closed. It was a sign I should have been relieved by, but I had already underestimated my surroundings twice today. Three times was not a charm I was willing to buy into.

I unlocked the door without knocking and barrelled in, Trudeau brandished.

11

A scream met my abrupt entrance.

"Ellie!"

I spun to the right. Rosalie stood there, gripping the place above her heart. Her eyes were bright with terror.

"Étienne!"

"He's asleep… Is that blood?"

"Not mine." I shoved past her, crossing the long corridor to the last door on the left. I opened it quickly, but quietly. Light broke from the hallway into the dark room, illuminating the sleeping form of my six-year-old son. He did not stir. A sound sleeper. Unlike his mother.

The relief that swelled through me was accompanied by exhaustion. The adrenaline was gone from me, and the pounding in my head was ever more prevalent.

I shut the door, holding to the knob as I swayed on the spot.

"What happened, Ellie?"

"Painkillers," I replied and hurried into my bathroom. The light reflected off the bluish-grey tiles, blinding me, and my head begged for reprieve. I reached for the bottle of pills that I had forgotten in the medicine cabinet, and ran the faucet. Counting to fifteen, I cupped the flowing water and downed it alongside two pills.

In thirty minutes, the headache would dull, but until then my vision swam black.

I needed to sit down. I needed to sleep.

Rosalie stood in the door, blocking my way and my needs.

"It's been a long night, Sally."

Rosalie Lavigne's spirit animal was a hen, of that I was certain. In the door frame, hands placed on her wide hips, she surveyed me with the most piercing sapphire eyes, like a mother reprimanding her child. She was only two years older than me, but that hadn't stopped her from taking on a maternal persona when she had discovered that I moonlit as a demon hunter. It had never been my intention, but I had been desperate for a permanent babysitter.

After everything she had done for me, the least I could do was give her a lowdown of the night.

So I did. But first I changed into something a little less blood-splattered.

We sat in my small living room, on the beige linen sofa that I had bought second hand at a flea market. The little mites had come with it, but a good spray had fixed that. Now, it was the comfiest thing I owned.

"Jesus, Mary, Joseph," Rosalie swore at the tale's end. "Did anyone follow you here?"

"I made sure not," I assured her.

"So do you think they know you live here?"

"I don't know."

"Is that what we're accepting?"

"For the moment." My headache was diminishing, but the fatigue was unrelenting.

"Can I make you tea? I'll make you tea."

Before I could decline, Rosalie was in the kitchen, running water into a kettle.

I stayed sitting, waiting for the painkillers to work magic. They proved much more effective at subduing my mind than Amaranth's sorcerer.

13

The tea that Rosalie delivered before me was even more relaxing. Blueberry almond flavor filled my stomach with delight and my head with ease.

"You need sleep. We can talk in the morning."

Rosalie's compassion worked the last of the magic in this consoling spell cast over me. I was ready to fall asleep where I sat. She deposited a woollen blanket over my body.

"You know where to find me if you need me."

"Next door," I murmured. "Thanks, Sally."

She left, and I stood. It was tempting, the idea to fall asleep there, but as exhausted as I was, the back of my head still stirred with anxiety.

I let myself into Étienne's room and crept towards him.

"Mon p'tit prince," I whispered, stroking his ebony hair. He didn't get that from me.

Hazel eyes opened up to stare at me, bleary at first. Those were mine.

"Maman," he whispered. "Is it morning?"

"Not yet. I thought you might like to sleep with me."

Despite the dazed look in his gaze, he reached for me.

I took him into my arms, wrapping him in the blanket.

He clutched me and I felt his love. My heart leaped into my throat, but a good swallow put it back in its place.

I carried him into my room, and we lay him down on the bed without unmaking it. I clung to him through the night, glad to know we were safe, and determined to make sure it stay that way.

CHAPTER THREE

A Trip

Demons exude the most repulsive scent, sulfuric and gag-worthy. The ignorant blokes of the world are unable to scent it, but those of us who know the truth of demons must deal with the smell. It took me three hunts before I found the strength to keep my meal down. It was one of my proudest moments.

- May 6th 1994

I could have slept in, but Étienne's waking motions broke through my resting state. The smell of strong coffee, honey and blueberries cemented the need for me to wake into the morning, beckoning me to rise and stumble after Étienne into the kitchen.

Rosalie flipped a pancake over the stove, and Étienne clapped his hands.

"Bon matin, Aunt Sally," he chimed.

"Bonne journée." Rosalie turned away from her batter to give him a quick hug. She threw a wink in my direction, then returned to her task at hand.

"Sleep well?"

"I could have slept more."

"There's coffee for you in the pot. That acrid stuff, dark and bitter as you like it. Should wake you right up."

"Merci bien!" I poured myself a cup and downed the contents. It worked well, dispelling the grogginess of my mind.

"May I have some, Maman?"

"You can stick to milk." I opened the fridge and reached for the carton. It was a brown colour. I shook it at Rosalie. "What's this?"

"Chocolate milk."

"Who's it for?"

Rosalie clucked her tongue—I mentioned the hen thing, right?—as she slid the cooked pancakes onto a porcelain platter. "Étienne deserves a treat every now and then."

"Étienne deserves a long life."

"I'd rather have the chocolate milk," Étienne insisted.

"Of course you would." In the end, I relented and passed him a small cup along with an orange.

I had almost forgotten my fear from the night before, but in this moment of bliss, it returned with all its force to remind me that these instances were now tenuous at best.

Rosalie hadn't forgotten either. As she served us her Greek yogurt blueberry pancakes, she asked Étienne, "Would you like to hang out with me today? We could go see that new superhero film."

"It's Sunday," I reminded her. The only day of the week I didn't work, I cherished this chance to spend time with my son.

"I know, I just thought you might want to take some time to look into that problem at work."

I snorted at her lack of subtlety. "Thanks. I'll take care of it tonight. Tomorrow's Étienne's first day at S-C-H-O-O-L."

"I can spell," Étienne muttered under his breath.

Rosalie smiled at him, then looked to me with an apologetic air. "I'd forgot."

"I wish Maman had."

"Maman's an elephant," I told him.

"I thought Maman was a lion."

That earned him a proud smile and a long kiss on the forehead from me. "And you are my cub," I whispered into his dark hair.

I needed this day to cherish with my son because, with the evening, I would be fighting to ensure it wasn't our last.

Our destination was decided by habit.

The train ride to Sainte Anne de Bellevue took almost an hour, but the travelling was part of the fun for both of us.

Étienne took the window seat as we rode, staring out at familiar scenery: greenery that blended into highway and rail-yards, then residential areas. It was the same sight every third Sunday, but Étienne could not be pulled away from watching the transformation of landscape and life.

While he surveyed our external surroundings, I held sentry over the interior of the compartment. There were only a few people riding with us. Most who had started the voyage with us at Lucien-L'Allier Station had already disembarked, but there was still a young teenage couple putting on some fine PDA, a man in his forties talking loudly into his smartphone, and an old woman knitting a scarf occupying the space with us. No one I would ever consider threatening. The most perturbing sight was the kissers.

Three stops from ours, they disembarked. In their place appeared a woman maybe a decade older than myself, distinguished by a purple streak that ran through her hair. She settled into the the seat a couple of rows ahead of us.

She carried with her a heavy odour of flowery perfume. I couldn't detect a demonic stench off her, but my brain whirred nonetheless, picking up a suspicious vibe. The feeling tempted me

17

to get off one stop earlier. There was always a bus we could catch to the small village. As the train slowed, I reached for Étienne's hand.

He looked up at me at the contact, eyes beaming wider than his smile.

"Could we…?"

The woman rose up and strode away towards the train doors.

"Could we what, Maman?"

"Nothing, mon p'tit prince."

I held onto his hand and stared out the window with him, watching the woman walk away without looking once towards us. The incident left me even more paranoid than I had started.

She wasn't following us, but I still felt a thrill of unease. Perhaps a Sunday outing had not been the best idea.

The anxiety stayed with me until we hopped off at Sainte Anne de Bellevue. Étienne's innocent exuberance was enough to bring a smile back to my face. I still kept my senses alert for anyone who might be trailing us, as he pulled me along to our preferred seafood place.

After a lunch of fish 'n' chips at the usual joint, we walked to the canal where some dozen odd sail and motor boats were moored in anticipation for the lock to fill. We had watched the event too many times to count on all forty fingers and toes, and yet Étienne's eyes were as round as ever, drinking in the sight. His hands gripped so tight to the rail that his knuckles turned white.

"Careful your circulation," I warned him.

His grip loosened, colour spreading again through his hand.

When the water level finally matched the river, the gates opened, and the boats cruised along to continue their passage along the Sainte Lawrence River.

"Maman, can we buy a boat?" Étienne asked as he always did.

"One day," I promised as I always did.

We bought some ice cream next and strolled around while we waited for the next train to take us back to the city.

"Could we move here, Maman?"

A trail of chocolate caramel dribbled along his chin. His tongue cleaned what it could reach. I passed him a napkin, and he dutifully wiped away the remaining blemish.

"Don't you like where we live?"

Étienne shrugged. I followed his gaze to the water, knowing what he was going to say next. His thoughts were mine. This quaint little area of town by the water was a place far lovelier and homelier than the bustle of Downtown Montreal.

"I like walking by the water."

"The river passes by Vieux-Montreal. And we're not so far from that."

"It's so noisy there."

"There's noise here too."

"It's different."

"I know." I sighed. There was no easy way to convince him of why we had to stay where we were: Maman hunts demons at night, and it would be murder to commit to a long commute back and forth.

"Maybe one day?"

My hand slipped onto his shoulder and gripped it tight. "One day."

The train ride back was quiet. Étienne fell asleep, his head resting on my lap. I held him close, stroking his hair, and knew that I would die for him if necessary. If quitting my night job could have better protected him, I would have. But he was safer with me stalking the streets for demons where I could shield him from the past that had brought him to life.

One stop from our destination, Étienne awoke and stretched with a yawn. "What are we doing now?"

"What would you like to do?"

"Could we go to the bookstore?"

"As you wish, mon p'tit prince." It made the bookworm in me smile to hear his request. It flamed my maternal ego too, assuring me I wasn't incompetent in all respects.

We walked to the shop on McGill Avenue and headed first to the young adult section. Étienne perused the shelves with a sharp eye and finally passed me a book from the 9-12 shelf.

The cover showed a girl wrapped in a blue cloak standing at the edge of a snow-covered town, the faint silhouette of a dragon cresting through the dark clouds above. The blurb on the back described it as an urban fantasy set in Tibet and a female protagonist with no memory of who she is or the powers she possesses. The promise of no sex, minimal violence, and female empowerment gained my approval on all three fronts, but I asked Étienne anyway, "Why do you want to read it?"

"Because there's a dragon on the cover."

Ah yes, my son: the precocious child.

I picked up a new contemporary release for Rosalie, one of those sappy romances that she devoured at night, and a dark fantasy for myself. There was something to enjoy in stories of demon-fighting women.

It was late enough as we left the store, but even if it hadn't been, I would have ended our day trip then.

Stepping out into the street, I caught a glimpse of a woman vanishing around a corner. The streak of purple was difficult to miss.

My grip on Étienne's hand tightened. I drew him closer to me and hurried to fall in step with the crowd.

I twisted my head back in time to see her come back around the corner, her head downcast. I looked away before she could notice me staring, assured that she had been the woman from the train.

We were being followed.

CHAPTER FOUR

A Stand

There are a number of ways to injure a demon. Holy water weakens them, words can slow them sometimes at best, but the surest way to kill them is to sever their head from their shoulders. I'm fairly certain that Joseph-Ignace Guillotin was a demon hunter in some capacity.

- March 15th 1994

My home. My life. My son. All of it was compromised. And it pissed me off.

The woman with the purple streak followed us all the way home. The art of keeping an eye on a stalker without the stalker knowing that they'd been discovered was far more difficult than just plain old stalking.

Whether or not I pulled it off was not anything I was going to worry about. My priority was Étienne, and getting him to safety.

A block away from our apartment, I gave Rosalie a call.

She answered halfway through the first ring. "Missing me?"

"I thought you might be missing someone else," I replied.

"Do you think I should be missing someone else?"

"Definitely."

"Maybe I am."

Rosalie was waiting outside our apartment when we arrived, an overnight bag slung over her shoulder.

"It's all set," she said.

"Are you going on an adventure, Aunt Sally?"

Rosalie winked at him. "And you're coming with me."

Étienne's eyes found mine, round and anxious. "Are you coming too, Maman?"

"Later. Aunt Sally will take you there; I just have some work to do first."

A pout crept across his lips, his eyes shining with disappointment. "I want you to come with us now."

"I know, mon p'tit prince. But this is important." I knelt down beside him and pulled him into an embrace. "Not more than you, of course. But sometimes things come up. And we have to deal with them even though we'd rather be with the people we love."

He just nodded, forgiving me, but not understanding. There was no way I could make him comprehend either. And it frustrated the hell out of me.

I helped him pack a small bag of things to bring with him, including his favourite stuffed toys and two books. I would assemble the rest of his things with mine when I was alone.

He hugged me once more before Rosalie led him away from me.

At the elevator, he turned to wave at me. I waved back, and my heart broke. My sadness wasn't long lasting, replaced by a deep ire that filled me with the desire to break something.

Tonight would be a good night for some demon killing.

Waiting for the bastards to show up required a test of patience. It gave me plenty of time to think and reflect.

I moved around the apartment, rifling for the items that contained the most value. Some trinkets I wouldn't be able to take with me. Like the scribblings on the wall that marked Étienne's

23

growth over the years. My fingers traced the lines and the ages inscribed beside them: three months, eight and a half months, one year… They continued all the way to his sixth year. Remembering didn't get me misty-eyed. It kept me furious.

My memories remained my only companion as the sun set outside the window of my apartment. The colours of the sky seeped into the living room where I sat, painting it in shades of red and orange. I waited impatiently, unable to keep still. My feet took me around the apartment enough times to make a dent in the floor. As I did, my craving for blood grew.

We do not crave the kill. It is a calling. Not a desire.

My father's words.

We are not murderers. We are protectors of the innocent. A heavy burden.

And more.

I walk these streets because my father did. And because his mother did before him. And her mother before her. And her father before that. It is a responsibility of our heritage. Will you bear it as your mark?

My father hadn't asked those questions so that I could choose my path. He had always expected the answer he wanted to hear. And I had always obliged: "Yes."

I often wondered what would have happened if I had said no. Would my father have died when he had? Probably not. But in that scenario, Étienne would never have been born. Because if my father was still alive, I would never have met—

The door banged open, rudely dispelling the rest of my thoughts. The abrupt entrance eased my irritation rather than aggravating it. I sank onto my couch, perfectly content, my Trudeau in one hand, Éponine in the other.

Four figures stormed in. They looked human, but their acrid stench was overwhelming. At the head of them, I recognized the woman who had followed us on the train. The perfume she had used to conceal her true identity was gone, and I could smell her clearly. She was flanked by two men and another woman. The latter wore a pixie cut, a ginger like me. Her hazel eyes were accentuated by the charcoal rims she had coloured her lids with. The two men were short and pudgy, they looked so alike they could have twins, but one had greying hair and the other thick chestnut locks. Ugly mugs made even more unpleasant in comparison to the two ethereal beauties they held company with.

Whoever had summoned them was a pig hyped on testosterone.

"I expected you sooner, so supper's already gone cold. I'd be happy to start the oven up again, but I'll need some fresh meat. Any volunteers?"

Purple Streak pulled a revolver from her coat pocket. It was the rarest sight. Most powerless demons didn't resort to human armaments in battle, preferring curses over missiles.

A bullet fired, lodging into the wall an inch above my head.

"That was a warning shot."

"Doesn't your Master want me alive? The last one did." My hand clutched the dagger tighter, ready for things to escalate quickly.

"Alive doesn't mean whole." She aimed her gun lower.

I moved before she could shoot again.

As I jolted forward, a blast of flames barely missed me, but I felt the heat as it passed to my left. The fireball collided with the coffee table, setting it ablaze. At least one of them was an Elementaire.

These demons were going to keep me on my toes. I flung Trudeau before another attack could come, glad that I had had the foresight to dip him in holy water.

It struck Goldilocks. He shrieked and burst into flames, his body scattering into ash.

One down.

Three to go.

I lunged with Éponine as another ball of fire came at me.

Charcoal-eyes was responsible for it. More flames flew even as I dodged the first onslaught. I ducked into the kitchen, leaving my wall to take on the brunt of both attacks. Scorch marks blackened it.

I didn't care to think how I was going to explain the damage to my landlord.

Behind the counter, I took a moment to catch my breath and consider my options.

I didn't even have that long.

A bullet shattered the glass vase that stood on the counter above me. I was showered with the debris. My skin bled where the shards sliced it.

"You need not face this pain."

I pulled open the drawer to my top right and deftly reached into it for my butcher's knife. The sharp blade gleamed as I held it before me, reflecting clearly that Purple Streak was approaching to my left.

With a great cry to summon my force, I stood up and threw the blade in her direction.

It caught her in the temple. She reeled back, stunned, but not decimated.

I leaped towards her just as she fired another shot.

I couldn't dodge this bullet and took it to my shoulder.

Raw pain exploded and threatened to pull me under. I fought the urge to collapse, the image of Étienne keeping me upright.

Éponine pierced her heart, and she dissolved into ash. The butcher's knife and the revolver both fell atop the pile that had once been Purple Streak. I reached for the latter.

Blood oozed from my shoulder, but I was not dead or dying too quickly. And there were still two demons left.

They had forsaken their guises for their true forms. Charcoal Eyes towered scarlet and scary. Baldy lumbered, a grey horned demon with a snout and potbelly.

Fire and ice shot towards me. I dove forwards, barely evading the attacks. The revolver in my hand pointed up to fire off one, two, three, four shots.

The bullets struck true, but the demons stood strong. Their decimation was a task for Éponine. She sliced through the air as the two demons wavered and hit her first mark.

Baldy evaporated, leaving the foulest stench in his wake. Already nauseous with blood loss, I gagged.

Charcoal Eyes screamed in frustration. Her hands rose up, prepared to strike me down.

I threw myself at her, not with the intent to kill, and knocked her to the ground. I somersaulted over her as we fell and positioned myself over her form. Éponine pressed into her neck.

"Tell me what I want, and I'll let you live."

"You want to know who sent me?"

"I do."

"Then kill me."

Why were demons such a stubborn lot? My irritation at her evasion fuelled the dark hatred in my gut. "A name for your life. It's a good deal."

She gripped my hand, and her fire burned against my flesh. With a roar, I carved Éponine through the skin of her neck and she disappeared into ash.

I fell to the ground, panting, my hand blistering, my shoulder bleeding. I was alive, but I knew nothing more about who was after me or why.

What I did know was that if I didn't take care of the bullet in my shoulder soon, it wouldn't matter for long.

The streets of Montreal were no less crowded on this, the Sabbath day in the Christian calendar. There were the same amount of lowlifes and degenerates, the same sinner to saint ratio—an estimated 3:1 in my book. Purveyors of lust, greed, and hubris mingled with conveyors of chastity, generosity, and humility. I weaved between the vices and the virtues in a grey world of moral ambiguity, bleeding to death.

The bandage I had wrapped in haste around my shoulder was soaked with blood. My coat concealed the sight from the world. On my other shoulder, I carried the satchel I had pinched off Amaranth the night before and a few well chosen possessions. It was an extra weight that slowed my pace. The wise thing would have been to leave it. Nostalgia lugged it along with me.

Walking was taking everything out of me, so I hailed a taxi and gave him my intended destination: "Saint Joseph's Oratory."

He was one of those drivers who knew how to work the streets to make the most profit. By the time we arrived at the great edifice, I was teetering dangerously towards unconsciousness.

I shoved multicoloured dollar bills into the driver's hand and stumbled out onto the streets.

The monstrosity of steps that led up to the white building adorned with a green dome was unavoidable. I ascended the stairs falteringly, the need to survive a driving force that kept me from giving in.

One man hurried to help me as I nearly took a tumble back.

He steadied me and then retreated as I waved away his good intentions. He must have believed me to be caught in a drunken stupor because he didn't redouble his efforts.

Alone, I made it to the lower entrance of the Oratory near the gift shop.

The space was filled with a mixture of religious fanatics and excitable tourists. I paid them no heed, making for the elevator.

By some grace, I found that I was alone in the lift as it descended to the bottom level.

The doors opened, revealing a cavernous space. Water trickled down the stone wall before me, the mugginess of the underground space greeting my emergence.

In the corner, a statue of Mother Mary loomed, a presence meant to comfort. A woman stood before her, both hands pressed against the marble feet, head bowed in deep prayer.

I hesitated on the spot, watching the woman offering her sorrows and struggles to the virgin mother of Jesus Christ and felt compelled to do the same.

I am a mother as you were a mother. Let me survive this night so that I may protect my son.

I was no Catholic. I held no religious affiliation, but in this space, I could believe in a woman who had given herself to a higher calling and hope that belief and intention were enough to save me this one time.

"Eléonore."

I half fell, half fainted into Sinéad's open arms. Confronted at last with an ally and the promise of safety, I collapsed towards the darkness calling my name without fully relinquishing to it.

She dragged me, my feet doing the bare minimum to help her bear my weight across the floor of the underground level of the Oratory, towards a remote area. I paid little heed as she slid aside a secret nook and gingerly manoeuvred us into the dimly lit staircase that led to her haunt.

Stronger arms took me from hers.

"You didn't mention a bullet," a gruff voice harrumphed.

"I did say I was dying," I moaned in turn.

"Can you save her?"

Sinéad's care-worn voice was the last thing I heard before the blackness finally stole me away from reality.

CHAPTER FIVE

A Safehouse

There are four levels to the demon hierarchy. At the bottom are the Faiblesse. The powerless. They rarely cross over on their own, always coming to serve a demon of a higher order. Snivelling little cowards for the most part, I'm never sure if I should pity them or relish in an easy kill.

- July 6th 1994

The pain of the bullet being dislodged from my shoulder jolted me from my unconscious.

I came to with a scream of agony that ended in a 'merde'.

"Language, Eléonore."

Tweezers held a bleeding bullet in front of my vision. If I had been squeamish, I would have fainted again. I wish I had been. It would have been nice to feel nothing.

Liquid poured over the open wound in my shoulder and the pain intensified tenfold.

The slew of profanities that left my mouth was a long list of every known sacred object in the Catholic religion.

"It's your fault for getting shot."

I grimaced at Bernard. A tall and husky man with a thick mop of hair and golden beard, his amber eyes were round with condemnation.

"That actually hurt a lot less."

"It's not going to get any better," he said and held up a needle and thread.

He was right.

I took the rest of the abuse of his healing technique without any further outbursts, finding strength in the hand that held to mine. Sinéad sang me a soft Gaelic lullaby while Bernard worked the needle in and out of my skin.

My eyes kept on her for strength. We had known each other since I was a child. She had become like a mother to me in the years when I had had none. A dark beauty, her black hair was streaked with grey, showing her age. Her emerald eyes hearkened her Irish heritage.

"Oh lass, you came far too close tonight to the other side." Sinéad's accent was as strong as ever, though she'd been living in Montreal for close to forty years.

"It's not something I want to repeat," I assured her through gritted teeth.

"No, as well you should not."

I remembered then the satchel I had brought with me. "The demon last night. I took something from her."

"I have it," Sinéad assured me, gesturing off somewhere I couldn't see. "I think it will not amount to anything too dangerous."

"I was what she wanted," I mused, glad to keep talking. It helped to distract me from the pain of Bernard's work.

"If I had known…" Sinéad sighed heavily. "I trusted someone. Their betrayal has been dealt with."

"Who?"

"They are no more, so it does not matter. What matters now is making sure you're in no more peril."

"Étienne—?"

"He and Rosalie are safe." It was Bernard who guaranteed this, finishing off his last suture and snipping off the hanging thread with his scissors.

"Thank you," I whispered, passing on my gratitude for his help in both healing me and housing my son. "Sally chose well."

"Will I be bringing you back with me?"

"Can we be sure that no one will find us...?" A gasp of pain escaped as I shifted a little, pulling me back towards the recess of my unconscious.

Sinéad placed her hand against my forehead and whispered a Gaelic word: *Misneach.* The pain in my shoulder subsided as she called for me to have heart. She passed me a cup. "To ease it."

I took a deep gulp of the liquid without questioning the offer. There was no one else I placed such trust in.

The effect was instantaneous. There was still an ache to be felt where my skin had been stitched back together, but it was far more bearable. I could imagine sleeping if I actually felt tired. But I was alert and teeming with irritation.

"I still don't know who's after me. Until I do, it might be better if I leave Étienne with you and Sally." The thought of being separated from my son was going to kill me, but then staying with him could mean sentencing him to death. I would find someplace else to spend the next few nights until I could figure out what was really going on.

"You need not worry for their sake," Sinéad assured me. "And you need not wonder for long."

"You know who's after me?" I shot up a little taller, glad that there was no pain to hold me back. My heart was racing with the need to know, my fists curling with the will to strangle. "Tell me."

Sinéad's hand clasped mine, and it relaxed in her grasp. "Not tonight, Eléonore. Go to your son. Get some rest. You'll be

safe with Bernard. After work tomorrow, meet me in the Garden.
I'll tell you then."

"It's a he, huh?" My instinct was to demand answers from
Sinéad, but if she promised we were safe, I would believe her.
"Bastard." I spat the word. The wad of saliva struck Bernard in the
face.

He glowered at me. "If I'm taking you home, you're
going to stop projecting bodily fluids, got it?"

"Yeah, but I have to warn you. I'm feeling a little
queasy."

Bernard drove with both hands on the wheel at ten and
two, his eyes straight on the road, his speed consistently set five
kilometres above the speed limit. I rode the whole way with my
head out the window, as per Bernard's orders.

"People can get decapitated doing this."

"Dogs do it all the time, and I haven't seen any heads
flying." Bernard's eyes never wavered from the road.

"Maybe I should bark, let my tongue wag."

"Whatever makes you feel more comfortable."

"If I don't wet the seat before we go home, do I get a
treat?"

"I'll even rub your belly."

He flicked his signal to indicate a right turn. When the
coast was clear, the Mini Cooper led us down a quieter street in the
Dollard-Des-Ormeaux neighbourhood.

"You know, even my grandma would say you drove like
an old lady."

"You don't have a grandmother."

"It was a figurative statement."

"I thought it was an insult."

"That too."

He pulled to a halt before one of the indistinguishable brownstone houses. Lights shone over the front door. Inside, the house was well lit too.

I glanced at the time on his clock. "Étienne will never be up for school tomorrow."

"You're still going to send him? With everything that's going on?"

"If they don't know we're here, they won't know where I take him to school. So yeah, my son's going to continue to live normally. I'm going to keep going to work. And tomorrow night, when Sinéad gives me the details on the son of a bitch who's messing up my life, I'll track him down and end him."

Bernard's eyes were wide open, shocked more than awed by my rant. "Okay, then." He stepped out of the car.

I was burdened with a raw anger that I half-expected would turn me into some kind of green rage monster. The more I dwelt on how my life had been turned upside down, the more the darkness in me built, wanting to destroy that which had destroyed, wanting to terminate the threat hanging over my son.

Rosalie stepped out onto the front stoop before we reached the first step. She dashed down the stairs to meet us, embracing Bernard and placing a big wet kiss on his lips. This second occurrence of PDA was far less offensive than the one on the train. Seeing their love calmed my rage. I wanted nothing more at that moment than to hold my son in my arms.

Rosalie ensnared me before I could go anywhere.

"Careful!" Bernard's voice resonated with mine as her hand came dangerously close to touching my shoulder. There was no pain anymore—Sinéad's concoction had worked a miracle on it—but I could sense the injury, and worried about any unnecessary contact to it.

"Oh, Ellie!" She hugged me tight, careful not to put any pressure on my wound. "Oh, Ellie!"

"I'm okay, Sally. Thanks to your fiancé."

"He's good for that."

"It's one thing at least." I winked at Bernard.

His eyes rolled. "You're lucky I've got me some thick skin and an elastic heart."

It was good to laugh and laugh we did until a tiny voice called our attention towards the house.

"Maman?"

Ignoring the fragile state of my shoulder, I shoved past Rosalie and Bernard. Scooping Étienne into my arms, I held him to me.

"We should get off the street."

Bernard's place was a homely one, marked by family photos, and comfy furniture. At two-stories it was larger than anything Bernard really needed for himself; in two years' time it would be perfect for the family I knew Rosalie wanted desperately.

Bernard bolted the door closed. "I'll be sleeping on the couch in the den." He gestured towards the room on his left. "Rosalie's in the guest room, so you and Étienne have the master's."

"Is this going to be our new home, Maman?"

"No, mon p'tit prince." I wouldn't tell him yet that we wouldn't be returning to our old apartment. He didn't need the stress of change, and I didn't need the stress of inventing a compelling lie. "Now, it's way past your bedtime."

"Mine too," Bernard chimed in. "My shift starts at seven o'clock tomorrow. I don't think my patients will appreciate me cutting them open on less than seven decent hours of sleep."

We bid our good nights, and I carried Étienne up the stairs. The master bedroom was a large space, coloured in green tones, dark and lush like a forest setting. It reeked of a man, but I could deal with the heavy musk for one night

Étienne jumped a few times on the bed. I was too tired to order him to stop. In five minutes, he was pooped anyway. Energy drained, he flopped onto the cover and lay there, spread eagle.

"Tomorrow's a big day for us."

"I still have to go to school?" His eyes were round with surprise, his voice thick with disbelief.

"Of course, you do."

"But we're on an adventure."

"Adventurers have to go to school. And mothers have to go to work."

He pouted, but his arguments stuck in his throat. I lay down beside him and gathered him into my arms. We stayed in that way for a bit, silent and pensive.

"Something bad happened tonight, didn't it Maman?"

My voice caught in my throat.

"Aunt Sally was worried. I could tell. And when Uncle Bernie left, he looked really angry. They told me everything was okay. But they were lying. I could just tell. They weren't smiling the right way when they said it. And they couldn't look me in the eye." He paused just long enough to take a breath then continued his tirade. "I knew something had happened to you. I knew it was bad. I asked Aunt Sally when you would be coming. She couldn't tell me. I thought… Maybe I wouldn't see you again."

I buried my head into my Étienne's hair, the pain in my heart so great I was almost sure it was going to break in two. "I'm always going to be here for you. Even if I have to leave for a bit, you don't have to worry. I'm always going to come back to you."

Étienne shifted in my arms, flipping over so that his eyes bore into mine, shiny and wet as they were. His hand fell on my cheek. "Promise, Maman."

"Promise, mon p'tit prince."

Mother Mary, if you're listening at all, please let this be one promise I can actually keep.

I had no hope that she would hear me, but I offered the prayer anyway.

Étienne snuggled closer into my chest. Assured of his safety and comforted by his proximity, I felt ready to descend into slumber. Before I gave into my fatigue, I sang:

> *Night's a-calling, the moon is high.*
> *The world is quiet, how dark the sky.*
> *Sleep's a-calling, time for bed.*
> *Your eyes are tired, rest your head.*
> *Do not fear, for as you do.*
> *I'll be close, holding you.*

My voice cracked; song had been my father's gift, not mine.

The sound of Étienne's snores convinced me that he was asleep. I soon relinquished too, drifting away into dreams that too quickly became nightmares.

CHAPTER SIX

A Façade

Demons draw their power from the night. The darkness fuels their strength and weakens the inhibitions of the humans they stalk. In the daylight, they are weaker and less compelled to stir up trouble. It's a good thing for us hunters, because the job really doesn't pay and we rely on a decently paying day job to get by.

- November 24th 1993

I stared up at the castle-like façade of Étienne's new primary school and was glad that I only had to worry about fighting demons.

Étienne's hand squeezed mine, tight enough to cut off the circulation. He had a strong grip that kid. It distracted me from the throbbing pain in my shoulder. Whatever concoction Sinéad had prepared for me yesterday was wearing off, but I had a bottle of painkillers ready in my bag for when the need became great enough.

"It's big."

"As big as it was when we visited last year, remember?"

"Nah, it's gotten bigger."

"Of course it has." In truth, I agreed with him. But then, the last time we had gone in I had known that he would be leaving with me too.

I watched other parents leading their children up the path to the building. Most said their farewells at the door. One boy, a scrawny tyke, was lying on the grass, kicking and pounding the earth, screeching even higher than a girl should be able to. He didn't

39

look big enough to have vocal chords that strong, but the ringing in my ears said otherwise.

Étienne ogled the banshee with wide eyes of dismay.

I knelt before him to draw his attention away from the scene, making him focus on me. "Mon p'tit prince, the first day of school is always the scariest. Because it's all new. You don't know what to expect. But you're brave, right? You can do this. I believe in you."

He smiled a little and gave the smallest of nods.

"And I'll be here when you're done," I pressed on, invigorated by the signs of yielding, "Waiting for you. We'll celebrate you being so courageous. Whatever you want. Ice cream. Pizza. Donuts."

"Pouding Chômeur?"

I had to laugh; my son, the dessert connoisseur. "If that's what you want."

His face brightened. Parents would say that bribery isn't the way to go with kids. In general, it wasn't something I liked to turn to either, but there was a fine line between a bribe and a reward.

I led Étienne without argument to the door. Together, we stepped into the building and walked the clean, locker-lined linoleum floor to the designated first-year classroom where a bespectacled man stood on the threshold. Tall, lanky, and bald, he smiled charismatically as we approached.

"Hey there. I'm Mr. Laurier." He addressed me first but introduced himself to Étienne.

Étienne extended his hand upwards. "Étienne Dormant. It's a pleasure. This is my maman, Eléonore."

"Well, you're quite the young gentleman, aren't you?" Mr. Laurier looked to me again, his smile full of laughter. He was probably well into his forties. Beneath round spectacles, his green eyes twinkled contentedly. A handsome man by my standards; completely off limit by them too. He shook Étienne's hand, then mine. "Étienne's in good hands."

The grip of his handshake assured me of the same thing. "Glad to hear it, Mr. Laurier."

I bent down once more and placed one last kiss on Étienne's brow. "Have a good day, mon p'tit prince. I'll see you this afternoon."

"I'll tell you about my day over Pouding Chômeur."

I nodded.

"Sounds delicious," Mr. Laurier declared, winking in my direction. "You have a good day, Ms. Dormant."

"And you."

"Bye, Maman."

I walked away and stumbled a little. Whatever Étienne felt at our parting, I believed that my pain was far greater. My heavy heart trembled with the thought of leaving him here. I wanted to believe he was safe, but that meant putting trust in total strangers. If something happened to him, it would be my fault. Even the pain in my shoulder couldn't compare to the ache inside. I quickened my pace to the exit before I could start to cry.

By the time I arrived at the Atwater Library, I was ready for it to be day's end. I was anxious to be with Étienne again and to set off to meet with Sinéad.

Inside, Catherine Fontaine was chiding teenagers. I nodded at my co-worker as I entered, my pace slow and reluctant.

41

I scurried to the back room to stow my lunch, then came back to the fronts desk where Catherine stood alone again.

A woman in her fifties, the only way you could tell was by the grey shade of her hair. Otherwise, she was the type of woman younger ones looked at and said, "I want to look like her when I'm that age." The definition of fit-spiration, tall and toned, slim and strong.

"I remember my first day with the twins. Maurice was no help at all with them. How did Étienne take it?"

"We're going for Pouding Chômeur after I pick him up."

Catherine's brow lifted, her eyes twinkling with bemusement. "A boy with good tastes. You two care for some company?"

"Rain check?"

"I'll hold you to it, Eléonore. Until then, care to do some heavy lifting?" She gestured at a stack of returned books waiting to find their home again on the shelves.

My shoulder cringed at the sight. I was going to have to turn to the painkillers soon. "I pulled something last night. Not sure I can."

"If ever you need, I have the best physiotherapist. I'll get you his card tomorrow. Check him out; he'll fix that shoulder right up."

She hefted the large pile of tomes in her muscled arms and strode off towards the shelves. Dejected, I watched her go. I preferred to be in the back with the books than at the front with the folks, but there would be no chance of it today.

I sat, hoping to be distracted but wanting to remain undisturbed. Caught in my own contradiction, my mind slid towards reflecting on the last two days and the hellhole of trouble I was slipping into.

I had made a lot of mistakes since that first night in Dominion Square that couldn't be undone. I would have to deal with consequences of my rash decisions. That was better done without worrying about whether or not I could have prevented this whole mess by reacting differently. I had to focus on working harder to avoid any more terrible outcomes.

I would let this day play out as normally as possible: lend books, charge latecomers, pick up my son, grab Pouding Chômeur, return to Bernard's, put Étienne to bed, visit Sinéad in the Garden, and get the name of the bastard after me. I could pause again then to determine a course of action. I expected to be done with this whole nonsense by the week's end. It was completely within the realm of possibility.

And for a couple of hours, it looked like I was right.

Only a handful of people came to bother me while I waited for Catherine to return. A group of teenagers borrowed research books—half of them probably wouldn't even bring them back in time. A woman returned some cozy mystery novels. When she asked if I had ever read them, I politely told her no and then had to listen to her long list of recommendations.

By the time Catherine finally returned, I was aching for a demon to hunt.

"So, how did you hurt your shoulder?"

"It's my fault; I was working too quickly. Should have been more careful."

"Words to regret by." She glanced at the clock overhead and heaved a sigh. "Well, it's gonna be one of those days."

Sinking into a chair, she pulled out a worn copy of *The Count of Monte Cristo*. "Guillaume is flying home this weekend from Prague."

"That's great! Maurice must be ecstatic."

"It's Gilbert who's really showing his excitement. He's been in a mood ever since his brother left. And he broke up with his girlfriend recently." She threw me a sideways glance over her book. "You should join us for supper one night."

"Maybe."

"You could bring Étienne. Gilbert loves children. Talks about having one of his own all the time."

Catherine was even worse than Rosalie when it came to subtext. "I'm sure he'll make some woman very happy one day."

Catherine harrumphed. "If only there were more nice girls like you in this world."

I smiled and avoided replying. If Catherine knew what I did for a living, her tune would be a lot sharper.

"Excuse me." We turned in unison, startled by the deep voice.

A man in a grey suit stood behind the counter, playing with his tie. Cleanshaven, hair slick with gel, he carried himself like one of the bourgeoisie.

"Bonjour." Catherine set her book aside and rose, but I stopped her with a hand.

"I got this one." There was no way I was going to let Catherine deal with this man. He might be able to fool everyone else with his fancy suit, but I could smell the sulphur pouring off him. "Do you need help with something?"

He leaned towards me. "I'm looking for a book."

I leaned forward in turn. "Do you know the title? Or the author?"

"Malleus Malleficarum." There were obviously a few people in need of a lesson in subtlety today.

"Ooh!" Catherine chimed. "Into the Wiccan stuff, are you? I just read a book on the Salem Witch Trials myself. Eléonore here doesn't have much of an appetite for it."

"There's no such thing as magic," I said as jovially as I could.

The demonic businessman laughed. "Maybe you should be the one helping me." He winked at Catherine.

"No," I asserted and placed myself defensively between the two of them. "I'd be happy to assist you in any way I can."

Catherine raised a disbelieving brow at me. I winked at her and mouthed, 'You're already married.'

"Oh yes, Eléonore is quite helpful. And dependable. A great girl."

I groaned inwardly but kept smiling as I came around the desk and accompanied my latest problem to an isolated shelf.

"A great girl, huh?"

"Shut up, demon."

"What gave me away?"

"What didn't?" I shot back at him but then reconsidered my tactic. We were in a public place. There were a lot of people who could get hurt if this demon wanted to cause a scene. Carrying a cocksure attitude about him that insisted he'd been around for a while; I could sense the power off him. Despite my earlier yearning, I would be relieved if this didn't end with bloodshed. "What do you really want?"

"I said, didn't I? *Malleus Malleficarum.*"

"What, so you can stick it up your ass?"

He sneered and glanced around the shelf. "Lots of people here today. And these books... Paper's remarkably flammable, isn't it?" He ran a finger along a book spine. A spark ran along it. There was no flame, but a tendril of smoke billowed warningly.

My hand fell instinctively into my jacket.

His hand shot out and restrained me. "I promise you, there's no need for that. Just point me in the right direction, and I'll be gone."

"Bullshit."

"You've got a mouth on you." He laughed hastily as a young woman appeared in the aisle.

She smiled at us, her attention turned to a shelf a few paces from where we stood.

"*Malleus Malleficarum?*" he asked a third time.

I didn't know what game was being played, but I didn't have much choice but to take part in it. I guided him away from the girl to the right section and passed him the book. It was decorated with a contemporary photo of a cackling witch. I wondered what the Puritans would have thought of the abomination.

"Thank you kindly."

We made our way back to the front desk where he proceeded to give his library card. It named him Alain Lawrence.

"Thanks again for all your help, Eléonore. See you in two weeks."

I watched him leave, bewildered for a moment. Even once he had passed through the door, I expected that he would return, leading an army of demons to kidnap me.

Then the reason for this all dawned on me. The truth of it struck me hard.

These creeps were all around me and had been for some time, watching my every move.

If I wasn't careful, I would lead them right to Étienne. The thought terrified me.

And then pissed me off even more.

I could not pick up my son from school. Whatever was happening, I had to believe that his current whereabouts were unknown. I had to believe that they were waiting for me to lead them to him, to provide them with the ideal bait. I wasn't going to be stupid—or rash—enough to do that.

By the time three o'clock came around, I knew what I had to do. In half an hour, Étienne would be expecting me to pick him up. For the second day in a row, I was bound to disappoint my son.

I pulled out my phone and sent a quick text message to Rosalie: *Won't be able to pick up, Étienne.*

Barely a moment later, an eagle's cry sounded.

Catherine started. "What on God's green earth was that?"

"Sorry." I glanced down at the message Rosalie had sent in reply: *What's wrong?*

Too many eyes, I replied to her.

When the eagle cried a second time, Catherine only raised a quizzical brow. "Everything alright, hon?"

"Yeah. Just forgot to ask Rosalie something."

I'll get Étienne. Just be careful.

"How is my Sally girl? Still engaged?"

"For now. Those wedding bells are pealing clearer than ever."

"Make sure she knows I'm expecting an invitation."

"I've seen your name on the list, no fear."

"Fantastique!"

It was. Étienne would be okay with Rosalie. If there was a problem, she would let me know. In the meantime, I had more messages to deliver.

At three fifteen, I bid Catherine a farewell. I would call her later tonight, after my little discussion with Sinéad, to ask for time off work. She would understand. Catherine was good for that.

"Enjoy that Pouding Chômeur for me!"

"Bien sûre."

I had barely reached the street when I heard the doors open behind me again. A quick glance back revealed an elderly gentleman and the young girl I had seen earlier in the stacks. I was less bothered that I hadn't realized her true form earlier than I was thinking of how many others were still in there.

They followed me, not taking much care to keep themselves hidden from sight. It was like they wanted me to know that they were there.

Even when I hopped onto the first bus that I could, they just strolled on casually after me and took seats at the front while I claimed one at the back.

I made eye contact with the girl. She winked in my direction. I scowled back, crossing my arms. It was my best attempt to look pissed off. It wasn't hard because I really was. But they didn't have to know that beneath my irritation brewed a plan.

CHAPTER SEVEN

A Bounty

Sorcerers have a hierarchy of their own: Ancients, Elders and Novices. For the most part, sorcerers are non-confrontational. But every once in a while, you get a jerk who decides he should use his power towards world domination. There haven't been any in my lifetime; still not sure if that's a blessing or a disappointment.

- December 3rd 1993

I led them up to Mont Royal. They never once tried to stop me or interrupt my path. Maybe they knew what I planned to do. Maybe they were hoping for a brawl too. As long as I chose the location for the showdown, I felt confident that I wouldn't be led into an ambush. I kept my eye on my phone, but there was still no word from Rosalie. It was the best of signs.

On such a beautiful day, the mountain streamed with people. I worried that they would become innocent victims in this, but my two pursuers trailed me without giving the people any notice. I was the only one who had anything to fear from their demonic wrath.

I could deal with that. Just not out in the open.

The leaves were changing colour, the green of summer giving way to shades of oranges, reds, and yellows. It was a vivid display of foliage that promised a changing of the seasons. They hinted at a sort of death coming. I hoped to add two more to the mix.

In the quiet isolation that the forest granted us, the sound of our feet crunching upon the leaves added an ambiance that I could relax in. A perfectly still and eerie setting. I couldn't have planned it better. Except that I probably subconsciously had.

Satisfied that we were safely distanced from civilians, I halted in my track.

"Hello, then," I said, spinning around.

They nodded in turn.

I slid Éponine from her sheath, then Trudeau from his pocket. "Who's first?"

"Aren't you tired of fighting?" the old man asked without flinching.

"I would think you lot are probably more tired of dying."

"Why not come with us?" the woman pressed.

"Why do we tell kids not to take candy from strangers?"

"You make a lot of jokes, Mademoiselle Dormant," a deep voice surprised me from behind.

I whirled around to see the businessman—alias Alain Lawrence—standing behind me. Where had he come from and how had he known that we would be there? The answer to those questions niggled me but pointedly evaded my mind.

"And I was so hoping we would run into each other again."

He reached into his bag and pulled out the copy of *Malleus Malleficarum* that he had taken out from the library. "It's interesting reading, but incredibly inaccurate. More fiction than fact."

He rifled through the pages. "We conclude, therefore, that the Catholic truth is this, that to bring about these evils which form the subject of discussion, witches, and the devil always work together, and that in so far as these matters are concerned one can do nothing without the aid and assistance of the other," he read the brief passage then laughed. "Oh, you humans have such funny ideas."

"Yeah, well, you'll have to forgive Kramer and Sprenger. They didn't know any better, writing as they were in the fifteenth century."

He slammed the book shut and threw it off into the woods. "Will you come quietly?"

"No."

Alain shrugged. As he did, his skin fell away, revealing an eight-foot tall turquoise demon beneath with six legs.

"Lovely," I murmured and brandished Éponine in his direction while keeping my peripheral gaze on the other two.

They had crept closer during our conversation but hadn't yet shed their skin.

Laughter echoed dimly, too close for comfort. Needles pricked against the skin of my arms. My body was trembling, not with fear, but with a desire for carnage. It was a darkness that built in my gut, and I did not try to swallow it down. It gave me energy, driving me forward to end the demons.

Three arms reached out for me. I dodged two and brought Éponine down against the third.

The demon shrieked. Blue goo sprayed from the wound. I shielded my face, then stabbed upwards with Trudeau, jabbing the blade into his belly.

His two comrades mutated into their true forms. They were the same bizarre six-legged creature, though smaller. One was grey, the other burgundy. They charged me and me them. Arms

51

reached for me, and I leaped, using the grasping limbs as footholds to propel myself up over their heads.

I would love to say that I then did the neatest little somersault in midair and cleaved one in half, but that would be exaggerating.

Instead, I came down on the ground behind them and missed my footing. I had never been very graceful. But I was quick.

Whirling around, I watched them stumble in their attempts to course correct. While they were occupied with that, I turned my attention back on Alain. He was in pain, but more than that he was furious.

He roared and hurtled towards me.

I ducked to the side, hearing the trampling of feet coming from behind me, and watched as the three collided into each other.

"Demon pile!" I shouted and leaped on top of their writhing forms.

Éponine came down once, cleaving off a grey head. Ash flew into the air.

She carved through the air a second time, claiming a burgundy head. Ash billowed again.

Alain screeched and raised an arm before I could do him in too. He caught me in the stomach, flinging me back onto the ground.

My shoulder roared in pain, and my eyesight went dark for a moment.

It was enough time for a hand to ensnare me. I was lifted into the air, his grip squeezing until the breath caught in my throat.

"You're lucky you need to be alive."

He squeezed again. I cried out before I could bite my tongue. Light danced in my vision. My head spun. Soon I would surrender to the darkness. It was already inside of me, growing, coursing through my veins.

Alain yelped and released me.

I hit the ground. There was pain, but the adrenaline that commanded me would not let my body slow down. I looked for Éponine. She lay in the dirt only a little out of reach. I lunged for her.

Alain was wailing, the hand that had held me disintegrating into autumn coloured leaves.

The sight caused me to falter. I whirled around, looking for an explanation. There was no one to see, nothing to provide a reasoning for it. I wasn't going to let it bother me.

Éponine severed the remainder of his legs from his body. Alain fell to the ground, a snivelling coward, grovelling for life.

"They won't stop coming for you," he hissed. "Let me live. I can protect you."

I hesitated, not considering his offer, but hoping to get some answers. "Who's your master?"

"I have none."

A freelancer, then. Less and less rare these days. "How did you know to come for me?"

"I saw your face."

"Who showed it to you?"

"No one."

"Well, I hope you like it."

Behind the pain in his gaze, bewilderment resonated.

"My face. 'Cause it's the last thing you'll ever see."

Like an executioner's blade, Éponine descended, and he was reduced to ash alongside his companions.

The wind stirred around me, blowing away the remnants. "Farewell, Alain the Slain."

I went with it, following it all the way to St. Joseph's Oratory and Sinéad. It was time to know what hellhole of trouble I was stuck in.

Sinéad was waiting for me in the Gardens of St. Joseph's Oratory.

The walk to the Oratory felt longer than it normally did. I had popped two painkillers, but they weren't working any magic on either my shoulder or head. I hoped Sinéad had more of her miracle concoction ready for me. If not, this shoulder was going to end me quicker than the demons.

I still hadn't heard from Rosalie. No news was making me anxious, so I reached for my phone.

Rosalie answered after just one ring.

"Where are you? What's going on?"

"I'm almost at the Oratory. I just wanted to check in, make sure everyone's okay. Make sure Étienne…"

"He's safe. A little miffed, but safe."

A little miffed. Rosalie was undoubtedly trying to protect my feelings. As long as he was safe, I could deal with his agitation… I had to hope, at the very least.

"Tell him I'll be there soon."

"Will you?"

"Uh-huh. Soon." I hung up with a promise to call back once I was done. I couldn't begrudge Rosalie her scepticism. If I had been in her shoes, I wouldn't have believed me either.

I marched into the gardens as the sun set in the distance, the dark hues of night falling over Montreal. The bright lights of the city cast a more luminous glow than the dim sliver of moon.

I followed the meandering pathway, casting occasional glances at the stone statues that marked the Way of the Cross. Sinéad would be waiting for me at one of them. I had a feeling I knew which, but I glanced at them all the same until I reached the thirteenth station: the Lamentation.

Undoubtedly inspired by la Pietà, the statue was one that depicted the Virgin Mary supporting the body of her deceased son in her arms. I would dare any mother to look upon it and not weep a little inside.

Jesus' form was limp, laid out upon her lap, while Mary bent over him, her hand cradling his head, her eyes cast with devotion upon his face. Behind her, the cross stood bare. It had been the last thing to hold her son's living body. Now she held him in death, mourning her loss.

I did not believe in much, but I was prone to believe in Mary's love for her son, and so I wept then with her. How she must have mourned for her lost son. To even contemplate her pain was an overwhelming exercise. My thoughts on the resurrection were more dubious, so I imagined that this time she held him was the last she ever had, her last opportunity to see his face, to kiss his brow—

Sinéad watched my emotions in silence, allowing me this time to grieve. I still had my son, but my fear for his safety was intense. It rolled over me like a wave, and I fell to my knees. I wrapped my arms around my chest, trembling as I cried without tears.

Eventually, Sinéad's hand fell upon my uninjured shoulder. "She will protect Étienne if you ask her to."

Sinéad was no more a Catholic than I was, but female empowerment and companionship was something that we trusted in and accepted as having power in this universe.

I took a moment to send a prayer to Mary, imploring her to watch over my son in those times when I could not. There was no answer, but I felt something move through the nature around me, and I took it as an assurance that my plea had been heard and that it would be done.

Rising, I turned to Sinéad. "Now, tell me about the bastard who's destroying my life."

Sinéad's smile curved with amusement, but her eyes shone with warning. "You should not seek to strike out with any rash action, Eléonore. It is not your death that is wanted."

She handed a folded piece of paper to me then. I took it from her hand and gave it a quick glance. A black and white photo of me stared back. It was perhaps three years old, but it was recent enough to still resemble me. Beneath it was written:

Eléonore Dormant
Location: Montreal, Quebec
Wanted ALIVE
Reward: C$500,000.00

I did a double take on the reward. That was a lot more than Monopoly money being offered. And all for little old me. I found it hard to believe that I could be worth that much to anybody, dead or alive.

"What is going on, Sinéad?"

A look of helplessness crossed her features. "If I knew, Eléonore... All I can tell you is that you are wanted. And the one who wants you is an Elder. Edmond Cartier."

I repeated the name a few times in my head, waiting for it to resonate, but there was nothing familiar about it. An Elder, though? I could be glad that it wasn't an Ancient. My chance of defeating a seven-hundred-year old sorcerer was nothing I would place any money on. Younger though Elders might be, their powers were strong enough. I'd had enough bad experiences with them to know that this wasn't going to be as black and white as I wanted it to be.

"And where can I find this Edmond Cartier?" I emphasised the French accent as I said his name; deriding ones enemy was a good way of limiting the fear of the threat.

Sinéad was less impressed. "I will warn you again, Eléonore. He might not be an Ancient, but as an Elder, he will have more power than you've had to face alone before. The last time…"

She stopped her sentence short, but enough had been said. The last time I had faced an Elder, I had been with my father and he had… The thought was there, but I wasn't going to dwell on it. The past was passed. My father was gone, and there was nothing to be done about it. But another Étienne was still alive.

"Maybe it'll be better if I'm alone."

"It is never better to be alone. Look how you've depended on your friends these past few day—"

"Once I've dealt with the Elder, that's all going to change. I don't need people's lives to be endangered because of me."

"Your father did not die because of you."

"Damn it, Sinéad!" I had hoped we wouldn't speak that point aloud. Dancing around it was acceptable, knowing it in the back of my mind was bad enough, but having to deal with the monster was untenable.

If Sinéad took offence to my expletive, she did not show it. Compassion was in her gaze and with it was a light of determination. "I know that you still carry the guilt, but you must release those poisonous thoughts. And you must not attempt to take on the sorcerer alone."

"You can't convince me of any of that. I've accepted what happened because of me. I don't want to relive it or reconsider it. I want to kill the son of a bitch and move on with my life. With Étienne. Now, tell me where I can find him."

"Not until you promise that you will not face him alone."

"And who would I take with me? You?"

"Not I. But there is—"

"Don't you dare say it!" My hands curled into a fist. There was anger burning inside me now. If she said his name, I would not be able to contain it. "He's not an option."

Sinéad bowed her head. She released a sigh teeming with disappointment that was strong enough to wash over me, placating my anger, but not swaying my mind.

"I can take care of this alone, Sinéad. I promise I'll be fine. For Étienne."

Sinéad met my eyes, but there was still doubt there. Despite it, she finally acceded: "Quebec City. That is where you'll find him. That is as much as I know."

She was lying, but I knew that I had gotten as much as I would from her.

"Thank you." I turned to leave.

"Before you go." She came around me to block my route and placed a vial in my hand. "For the pain in your shoulder. Two drops every twelve hours should do it. But no more than that."

Gratitude flowed through me, the pain in my shoulder easing with the mere promise of a cure.

She embraced me tenderly. "Come back to us, Eléonore. And do not be afraid to ask for help. You do not need to face these dangers alone."

I kept my reservations silent. I was glad for the friends I had, really and truly. But hunting was a solo thing. Alone I would go to Quebec and kill the damn sorcerer.

Alone I could guarantee that no one else got hurt.

I was prepared to leave for Quebec City that night, but not before seeing my son one last time.

Arriving on Bernard's stoop, I was not empty-hand. I bore gifts I hoped would gain me favour in my son's eyes.

Rosalie opened the door.

"Ellie, I've been so worried!"

"Where's Étienne?"

"In the kitchen." She eyed the bag in my hand as she ushered me in. "A peace offering."

"Do you think it will be enough?"

Mother Hen clucked her tongue.

Étienne looked up as we entered. His eyes were dark with anger and—even worse—disappointment.

"Mon p'tit prince—"

He stood up and ran past me. His feet drummed up the stairs, pounding in frustration. A door slammed overhead.

"Guess he's mad at me," I choked out the words.

"Give him time."

I shook my head. There wasn't time to give. I couldn't linger there longer than an hour.

59

The master bedroom door was the only one shut. I rapped on it gently. "Can I come in?"

"No."

I opened the door anyway.

He glowered at me from the bed, his arms crossed. It was amazing how much he looked like my father. And his.

"I said no, Maman."

I held my parcel out. "I brought us some Pouding Chômeur… If you're still interested, that is."

His eyes glowed bright, excited, but dimmed too quickly to stick. "You're bribing me."

How was it that my six-year old was able to use words like that? "Apologising. I wanted to be there—"

"Why weren't you?"

I lowered my hand. The real answer was easy, but I didn't want to give it to him yet.

"Can we eat and talk?"

He nodded and scooted over a little, an invitation for me to join him.

I sank down and retrieved the two cartons of dessert I had purchased. A sponge cake sat in a lake of maple syrup and caramel and smelt like heaven. Pouding Chômeur. *Poor Man's Pudding.* A dessert that required few ingredients and tasted oh so good.

He took a bite and licked his lips contentedly. I mimicked him, and we laughed. The tension eased for that brief interlude, then returned.

"Why didn't you pick me up?"

"I wanted to—"

"But you didn't. Why?"

I considered Étienne's eyes; they were wide, waiting for truth, hoping it would explain away my abandonment of this evening. Knowing that I couldn't provide either burdened me with guilt.

"I don't want to lie to you, mon p'tit prince, but I can't tell you why. Can you believe that I would have been there if I could have?"

His immediate response shone through his eyes: uncertainty, doubt. He looked away from me and spooned another helping of Pouding Chômeur into his mouth. When he looked up again, a dribble of caramel was running down his chin.

I stopped the mom in me from pointing it out. He licked it up with his tongue.

"I can," he conceded in a quiet voice.

They were the words I wanted, but they weren't delivered with the tone I hoped for. So soft and fragile, each broken promise was creating a shield within him, making him wary of blindly trusting my word. If I wasn't careful, the wall would become too sturdy for me to slip through one day.

"Can you forgive me?"

He nodded.

"Thank you." I reached for him and pulled him into my arms. He didn't react at first, but his arms at last wound their way around me.

He pulled away sooner than suited me. "Will you tell me one day, why you didn't pick me up?"

"One day." I cleared my throat. The last few minutes had been brutal, but the most difficult part was still to come. "Étienne, I… I have to go away for a while."

Étienne's face reverted to an anxious state. "When?"

"Tonight."

"Maman…" Tears glittered in my son's eyes.

"Just for a few days. I promise. And then I'll be back, and we'll get back to normal life."

He turned away from me, his back acting as a barrier between us. My hand found his shoulder, but he shook me off.

"If I didn't have to, I wouldn't. But I have no choice."

"Why is everything changing, Maman?" He turned back towards me, his eyes dry but accusatory.

"It's normal for things to change. And hard," I tried to reason with him.

"Really hard," he agreed.

He placed his dessert aside—all that was left of it was a puddle of syrupy goodness—and crawled over to me, clambering onto my lap.

His arms wrapped around my neck, his head nestling into the crook of my arm.

I rocked him softly. "I don't want to leave you again."

"I believe you." The trust was back; his eyes brimmed with it. "Can I come with you?"

"Not this time. But maybe the next."

"Will you bring me back a present?"

I laughed and kissed his brow. "Yes, mon p'tit prince. I'll bring you back a wonderful present." He deserved nothing less for what I was putting him through, for what he would still have to go through if I returned…

When I returned…

If I returned.

CHAPTER EIGHT

A Memory

The Tenebres rank above the Faiblesse and are the most likely to cross over to our plane to spread discord and disunity. In our world, they feel more powerful than they ever can in Daemoniar. Like the youngest child in a large family, the Tenebres have nailed down the rebellious stage with no sign of growing out of it.

- July 10th 1994

The trip to Quebec City was disastrous.

My first mistake was travelling through the night. My impatience and ire were ideal fuel for reckless decision making. Which, in turn, was a pretty sure way of getting killed.

My second mistake was choosing to take my father's old Jeep CJ5—affectionately named Marianne. It once had been—in its prime, that is—a fire engine red. Worn by age and demon attacks, it boasted a dirtier colour and a faded shade of that. It was still in working condition. Ten years ago, I had locked her away, learning to rely on my feet and public transport to work my way around the city.

I couldn't take a bus to Quebec City, and there was no chance of walking, so I had to return to her. A few blocks away from the storage facility, I became aware that I was being tracked.

The two demons following me were not the most subtle creatures I'd ever encountered. They made more noise than they probably realized and their stench carried across the north blowing wind, assaulting my nose with an acrid citric scent and chives. Not a pleasant combination.

I halted in my tracks and felt the anticipation bristle through my pursuers, eager for a fight. I was eager for it to be done. Turning, I flung a single dagger, impaling one. It faltered, but did not dissolve. I would need Éponine for that.

While the second mutated into a blue monstrosity, gangly and lanky, I lunged at the first and sliced him into dust with three carving strikes.

His partner towered over me. A clawed hand swept in my direction. I dodged the attack, leaping left.

I thrust out with my blade again and sliced the demon's side, drawing blood but not reducing it to cinder. Decapitation it was.

I glanced up. "Hey, big guy: mind leaning over a little?"

The demon stretched upwards, his form elongating. He reached for me again, and I ducked left, but he was ready for me, and before I could react, his other hand collided with me, flinging me back. I crashed back to the sidewalk. My body ached in protestation, bruised but not broken.

I shook off the dazed sensation that otherwise would have kept me down. My eagerness for a fight receded. The challenge of this engagement was annoying me more than a tad. I was impatient for it to be done with, so I sheathed Éponine and reached for a bottle of oil. I chucked it at him; the glass shattered over the demon's head. Liquid dripped down his face, a snarl broke from his lips. An orb of power formed in front of him, ice crystals defining the edge.

Two elementals in one day; I should have felt honoured.

I dipped one dagger blade into an extra bottle of oil. With a flick of a finger, I drew a flame from a lighter. The blade ignited as fire met oil and I launched it through the air.

It connected with the demon and fire shot out across its front. The ice ball vanished into thin air, and the demon released a loud roar of pain. He crashed to the ground on all fours and screamed again.

The shriek nearly created pity in my heart. Nearly.

Rising up, I marched to the demon's side and brought Éponine down in a slicing arc, severing head from body, reducing my adversary to ash.

I hesitated only for a moment over my most recent victim to retrieve the dagger. It would serve me no more, also having been reduced to cinder. I did not like the idea of being down one weapon, but there was nothing to be done about it.

Marianne was waiting for me in the garage, a layer of dust coating her. I did an annual check-up on her every year to make sure she was still running, but otherwise we were estranged individuals. It dawned on me that I hadn't yet undertaken this year's inspection. Too late to bemoan that.

Clambering into the driver's seat, I settled the key into the ignition. A turn of the hand and the engine revved up, puttering a little at first than smoothing out.

A sigh of relief fled my lips.

I gripped the steering wheel and leaned towards the dashboard. "Alright Marianne, you listen to me. I have to make it to Quebec City tonight. Can you do that for me? Can you get me there tonight?"

I took her silence as a reply in the affirmative and shifted gears to drive.

Marianne jerked forward, then again. I held tight to the steering wheel. If she wasn't going to get me out of here like I needed her to…

I didn't have to worry, though. Another jerk and she evened out, guiding me out of the garage and onto the dark street. I didn't appreciate then the danger that I was directing myself towards. I understood that the monster at the end of the road was an Elder sorcerer. I understood that the battle we were going to engage in would require one of us to die. I understood that I had to be victorious. But I didn't understand yet the real hellhole of trouble that was coming for me and my son. But I'm getting ahead of myself.

To recap, I had made two mistakes so far that night: leaving in the night and choosing my father's jeep. My third mistake was still waiting to be made.

I filled the first third of the drive to Quebec City with tunes on my dad's tapes and reminisced on the past. The combination of memories of old days hunting demons with him and sappy '80s ballads were enough to ease my frayed nerves. In its place, rose a nostalgic sentiment that dulled my senses.

The threat of emotions invoked by my remembering hindered my vision. Shutting off the music did little to break the curtain of sadness that commanded my mind. And nothing could stop me then from reflecting on the night my father had died…

The night had been darker than the present one. Thick clouds promising storms cloaked the moon and the stars.

We are driving down the highway between

The radio had been blaring, the music playing a classic rock piece. The guitar solo swelled over us, each strike of the drum resonating like the thunder that would soon come to ensnare the sky.

*We are singing along, my dad and I. He's
smiling while I air guitar the hell out of
one of his favourite tunes. We do not see the
demon darting through the darkness behind us.*

By the time we do, it's too late.

*My father presses hard on the brake and the
Jeep veers left. The demon barrels past us,
misses us. My father straightens the wheel once
more and slams down on the pedal. We shoot
forward. He rams into the demon, and it
evaporates into ash.*

It's clear that we're in a hellhole of trouble.

A car zoomed by, horn blaring. A middle finger cursed us. I had wanted to keep driving, but my father worried about the innocents that could get injured when this turned worse. By the time the next car had come along, my father was dead.

*We pull off, and a sorcerer manifests
through the stillness, suddenly and
silently. My father draws me behind his
body, instructs me to return to Marianne. I
refuse to go.*

This rebellious decision kills my father.

My father had tried to protect me, and he had died to do it.

*My father begins an incantation. We do not
have magical powers, but we have words.
They are blessings to dispel curses. Words that
reach to the goodness of life to break the
threatening evil. Not commands. Requests.
Sometimes the earth responds.*

That night it does not.

The first strike of lightning had shot from the sky. The roll of thunder that had followed wove terror in my heart. The sorcerer had laughed as the darkness of the night was illuminated. His magic was charged in storms. He had known it would be there. He had chosen this night because of it. He had targeted us.

*The sorcerer's first blast of magic forces
a divide between my father and myself.
Trudeau is in my father's hand as he*

launches forward. The sorcerer flings him
aside easily. His eyes meet mine. I am
afraid of what I see there but determined.
And reckless.

I make a move that decides my father's fate.

My weapons of choice that night are a
pair of silver hilted daggers. They were a
birthday gift from my father.

The last one I ever receive from him.

I fling the first at the sorcerer. He deflects it,
but I am already moving forward, and I am
upon him before he can react. My blade
sinks into the flesh of his belly, and I am
sure that I will kill him. I retrieve my
dagger. Raise it up to bring it down again.

The pungent taste of precipitation had been thick, but there was no rain that night. The humidity had held for another day. The next time it had rained was on the day my father was buried.

The sorcerer projects a force field, and I
fly back, colliding with Marianne's hood.
I am aware of a pain in my back and my
father calling my name. I am aware of
the sorcerer summoning magic. I am aware
that his power is already pressing against

69

*me, slowly suffocating me. I am aware that
his next attack will kill me. I am aware that I
will die.*

I know that I should be afraid. But I'm not.

*I am not aware that my father is running
towards me. I am not aware that the fear
running through him is the strongest he has
ever felt. I am not aware that it is not my
destiny to die that night. I am aware of the
sorcerer's blast of lightning. And finally, I
am aware that my father throws himself in
front of me. A human shield, he takes the
brunt of the blast.*

It kills him instantly. It is still killing me.

The night had turned deathly silent. Lightning still
illuminated the dark, but there had been no thunder to rumble in its
wake.

*I make my way to my dad's dead form. The
pain in my body is bad enough, and I know
that something is broken. But my heart is
shattered. And the pain of that is worse than
anything else.*

I want to die. I look to the sorcerer, hopeful.

There had been a bright flash of light and a second Elder had appeared. He had come to help my father. He had come too late. And I had fainted then, unwilling to deal with the pain anymore. But I hadn't died.

I knew what happened next only through hearsay. My rescuer had killed the sorcerer who had killed my father. And then a car passed by. The man pulled over, called 9-11. The paramedics determined the cause of death to be a heart attack. Idiots.

A car horn brought me back to reality just in time to realise that I was veering into oncoming traffic.

I jerked hard on the steering wheel just in time to avoid a head-on collision with an eighteen-wheeler. I caught the flash of his middle finger jutting out the window in my direction.

Two mistakes had already defined this trip. Leaving in the night and choosing Marianne as my vehicle of choice. The former because it had increased the chance of attack, the latter because it had left me vulnerable to memories.

The driver's gesture had caught my attention and my gaze refused to turn away until the truck had passed from my vision.

That was my third mistake.

By the time I looked back to the road ahead of me, it was too late to avoid the moose that stood blinded in my headlights.

CHAPTER NINE

A Struggle

Elementaires are second-tiered in the demon hierarchy. Sorcerers tend to summon them the most. The obvious reason is for the powers they wield over the elements for which they are named. Of course, the other reason falls on tradition. The first demon summoned was an Elementaire and so sorcerers continue to honour it because no one ever went astray making decisions based on an old and outdated practice.

- August 3rd 1994

I tried my best anyway.

My foot slammed on the brakes, my hands jerking hard on the steering wheel. Marianne veered right in a desperate attempt to avoid hitting the majestic creature and killing both of us in the process. The screech of her tires filled the air, a grating sound, like a child crying out in fright.

Old though she was, Marianne stayed upright. But my turn on the wheel led us into the ditch, and I jarred to a halt there, my forehead banging into the steering wheel with enough force to make my vision go black.

One.

Two.

Three.

Four.

Five.

Six.

Seven.

The blackness receded, and I came to again, hot blood trickling from where my skin had split over my left eye. It dripped into my already blurred vision.

The world was spinning in front me, a dizziness invading my mind. There would be no chance of me driving any further; I would be lucky if I could stay awake long enough to get some help. I would be lucky if it were only a minor concussion.

Car headlights flashed behind me, and I turned toward the direction of Quebec City. Illuminated in them was the moose I had swerved to save.

Except it wasn't a moose.

It was a demon.

And there wasn't just one anymore.

There were a dozen.

And they were coming towards me, branching out to surround me.

I stumbled onto the grass, Éponine drawn. I teetered, nearly fell, and shook my head, trying to regain my balance.

"Stop spinning," I shouted at the world; a futile command.

Nausea rose quick, and I threw up beside Marianne.

Three mistakes I had made. One reckless decision after another. One act of stupidity followed by an act of stupidity followed by another act of stupidity.

I thought I saw three princesses dancing in the background, one in a coral, one in periwinkle, one in daisy yellow.

I blinked, and they were gone. I was glad for the sight of the demons in their stead.

The ground shook beneath my feet, and I fell. The world was revolving again, a kaleidoscope of rainbow colours ensnaring

73

me. I was going to pass out again, and the demons would get me and then Étienne…

Étienne needed me to stay awake. Étienne needed me to beat these demons.

Those thoughts forced my body to rise. They planted my feet upon the ground. They kept my vision from going black. They kept me strong.

"If you want me," I addressed the crowd that gathered around me, "Then you'll have to come and get me."

They didn't wait for a second invitation.

At once, all twelve converged. Éponine sliced through the air ahead of me. She claimed three victims before the wall of shadows bore down upon us. I dove away, rolling under Marianne and tried to think.

The splitting pain in my head was not making it easy.

I had three options before me.

First, I could let them take me to the sorcerer and worry about destroying him once I was there. Downside: I wouldn't get the reward money myself.

Second, I could go down guns blazing, give myself a chance to cut down as many demons as I could before they took me in. Downside: same as above.

Third, I could try an exorcism. Downside: there was no guarantee it would work and same as two above.

I began to mumble in Latin as long spindly fingers reached out for me, creeping beneath Marianne, scrambling to pull me out.

I kept yammering on, spewing Catholic banishments, Islamic begones, and Hindu dismissals. All to no avail.

A hand found its way to my leg and yanked me out into the open before I could resist.

Éponine penetrated the gut of my capturer, and it dissolved into dust. Where it had been, three more came to take its place.

From one, a sheen of silver silk shot forward, tying my hands to the ground above my head. I tried to free them, but they were stuck good and strong.

They had defeated me, but I was not defeated. I still had words. From my lips, I renewed my commands for the demons' destruction. This time, I appealed to the Mothers. To Mary. To Hagar. To Devi. Even to Hera.

The demon nearest to me shrieked out, an agonised cry that evaporated. The embers of its obliterated form sprinkled upon the demon to its left. It too was blown into the next dimension. Unfortunately, it didn't take any of the others with it.

But someone had responded to me. I was trapped with my hands bound, but it felt good to know that someone had heard my plea for help and done something about it.

The earth beneath me trembled. It wasn't just my imagination this time. The roots of a tree broke the earth on either side of me and encased my body.

"Shut your mouth, woman."

The demon leering at me was a dark green shade. Its clawed hand curled into a fist, and the roots twisted around my body. Any more and they would break through my body.

"Doesn't your boss need me alive?"

"Alive doesn't mean whole."

"So I've been told—" The tree flattened hard against my throat, cutting off my wind and my words.

I sputtered, struggling to breathe.

"Take care, Gaiar. These mortal bitches are not strong. "

"I know that."

Their voices were dim in the back of my head. My body was searching for air to keep it awake. Without it, it would succumb to darkness and then death…

A bright flash of light illuminated the space around us, too effervescent to be the headlights of a car, too pure to be a lightning flash.

The root released me and air swept through my lungs. I choked as a drowning girl released from the ocean's grasp. My vision cleared. A jet of red light speared the green demon, and he burst into flames. Three other demons were felled with him, caught in the wrath of the flames that had claimed their comrade.

The roots slipped back into the earth, releasing me as they were liberated of Gaiar's command.

Multicoloured streaks filled the air while the cries of vanquished demons resonated in an inharmonious and unholy chorus.

Silence and darkness returned simultaneously, and I rose up from the ground. With Éponine in hand, I turned to look for the person who had saved my life, aware that they could be my foe.

In a way, they were.

My arms went slack. He had come again. As he had that night ten years ago.

The most beautiful eyes I had ever seen stared back at me. It had been six years since I had last seen them. Big and sapphire blue they beheld me, revealing amusement and a protectiveness that made my knees go weak.

Why is he here?

He had saved me, but I wished he hadn't.

Why is he here?

Had Sinéad sent him after me? I would be so upset with her if she had.

Why is he here?

We had agreed to keep our space. Six years ago, we had committed to separation.

Demons I could deal with. But not him.

Not Étienne's father… Not Raphael.

CHAPTER TEN

A Deal

- November 6th 1994

It was amazing how six years of separation had managed to aggravate both my hatred for the man and my lust for him.

Facing him at that moment, I felt compelled to ravish him and then slice his throat. I also felt like I was going to be sick.

Of the three, the last was the only one that I would give into that night. And did. Right then.

"You've been hurt."

"Stay away from me."

"I can heal you."

I straightened my posture, wiping a hand across my cheek to remove the smear of puke that was there. "I don't want your help."

"But you need it."

"I can take care of myself."

"A moment ago you were being suffocated by a tree."

Raphael strode forward, too quick for me to evade him. I blinked, and he was by my side, forcing me to sit.

I shoved him off, cursing him as I did with as many profanities as my mind could conceive and then some. The effort proved too much, and I faltered on the spot. The world revolved, the kaleidoscope of colours marring my vision once again.

Raphael caught me as I stumbled forward and eased me onto the cold ground. I tried to push him off, but my energy was gone. As were my senses.

"Will you let me heal you?"

I swallowed down the urge to throw up in his face. Admitting that I needed help was going to kill me, but not quicker than my injuries. "Everything but the shoulder," I agreed at last.

"Why?"

"Just leave it."

His hands hovered over my body, moving the length of it back and forth. I felt his magic swell through me, but never once did it touch the bullet wound. I could appreciate his respect, though he would never understand. It was my consideration of Bernard that obliged me to keep the scar of the attack. He had healed me, I couldn't have anyone else remove his mark.

My head was the last thing to feel his power. As he healed my concussion, everything became clear again. The drive for sex and death was no longer there. The world was still and dark. And Raphael was leaning over me, close enough to kiss.

I shoved him back. "Thanks."

"Anytime."

"Just this once," I corrected him, standing before he could try to offer me any help with that too.

With this new clarity, I took the opportunity to do a proper once over of the man I had once loved enough to take to bed, to conceive my son.

He looked taller and a little older than I remembered. That was just an illusion, though. Raphael was well into his three hundreds. His hair was still black, thick and curly, though not as long as it had been. The scruff around his chin was a nice addition to his rugged features.

His fitted purple shirt accentuated his toned form beneath a loose black vest. His dark jeans were equally flattering on him, tucked into the tall red rain boots I had bought him eight years earlier.

I despised how great he looked.

"You're looking amazing too, Léo."—Did he have to use that old pet name and read my mind too?—"Considering what you've been through."

"Well, you don't have to worry about it anymore. You've done your good deed. I'll call you again in six years."

I turned my back on him.

He was standing in front of me.

I had forgotten how annoying that could be.

"I don't have time to play games, Raphael. Get out of my way."

Raphael folded his arms over his chest and took a deep breath in so that his whole form expanded. He was already taller than I was—5'11 to my 5'5—and I felt dwarfed not only by his height but by the aura of magic emanating from him.

Starting a relationship with an Elder was one of the stupidest things I had ever done. Ending it one of the smartest.

"I have no patience left to be tried. I don't know why you're... Oh no." I did know why he was here. There was really only one reason for it...

"Sinéad sent me after you."

"She told you what happened?" The wry smile that curved his lips brought up a much more disturbing revelation. "You told her about the bounty?"

He nodded. His smug shrug and glinting eyes made me wish that he hadn't decimated all the demons in the vicinity. I could do with one to kill. "Just because we promised to stay away from each other, doesn't mean I haven't been watching over you. Over Étienne."

"If you ever come near him—"

"I never did and I won't," he asserted, but there was a wounded look in his eye as he said it. "But maybe…"

My eyes flared.

"I won't."

"Good."

"As long as you let me help you."

Éponine was in my hand before I even realized that I was drawing her from the sheath. "Is that a threat?" The tip of the blade pushed into Raphael's chest. He retreated a step.

"Only so that you'll let me protect you. C'mon, Léo. You want to get home to Étienne, right? I just want to make sure you do too. Nothing else."

"I can do this on my own. And I will." I kept Éponine pointed at him as I backed towards Marianne.

He did not move or disappear. Only watched me with a pensive stare.

"I get it. I do. Part of what happened that night was my fault too. I didn't get to him in time, and I hate myself often for that. But not as much as I'll hate myself if I fail you." His words implored with enough regret in his voice to cause me to falter. It was enough to break through my defences and resolve without shattering them.

I considered his offer, despite my better judgement. My instinct was to refuse him, but I could be enticed if the proper caveats could be arranged.

"You helping me wouldn't change the way things are."

"As expected."

"And I'd get to make the final kill."

"I have enough blood on my hands."

"And you'd have to follow my orders."

A sly smile curved his lips. "Wasn't that how we always did it?"

He had a point. I had always taken the lead during our hunts. There was a part of me that was thrilled by the idea that we could recapture times that I had once relished in. My better judgement told me that agreeing to this would get me into a whole different hellhole of trouble on top of the one I was already stuck in. Sometimes I could be such a glutton for disastrous decisions.

"Shake on it."

His hand took mine. It was warm, soft, and sturdy. It promised at once strength and courage and protection and love.

Yep. A whole hellhole of trouble.

CHAPTER ELEVEN
A Dilemma

All Novices can become Elders, but not all Elders can become Ancients. The deciding matter is one of birthright. The one thing that sorcerers share with humans is an incredible amount of intolerance. The elitist bastards only allowed the first female sorcerer to join their ranks in 1946. At least Québec gave women the right to vote in 1944. We humans have our priorities straight.

- December 16th 1993

Daylight was barely breaking across the sky when we finally entered the streets of Vieux-Quebec. Raphael had refused to let me drive. Just in case. I had refused to let any conversation pass between us. Just in case. We had arrived in one piece, so at least that was two good decisions in a night otherwise defined by bad mistakes.

"Drop me off at the nearest hotel."

"You're better off at my place," Raphael refused. "There's a guest room," he assured me before I could protest on the foundation of 'a disaster waiting to happen.' "And guaranteed safety. My wards are the best. No demons will find you there. C'mon, Léo."

I was quick to acquiesce to this suggestion, only because I was exhausted and ready to fling myself on the nearest bed to crash, and because of the money it would save me. It would only be for one night anyway.

He directed me to one of about thirty quaint two-floor houses cramped together on a cobblestone street. It was too late and too dark for me to appreciate the historical ground that we were trespassing on, but I was aware that we were in the heart of Canada's origins and I felt the weight of it as I followed him into his apartment.

It was not bigger on the inside.

His four-and-a-half flat consisted of two bedrooms, a bathroom, a kitchen and a den. He pointed out all five with a brief turn in the small hall that connected them all together and then guided me into the guest room.

"If you really feel the need, there's a lock on the door. I won't be able to come in."

I stared at him with narrowed eyes. "Do your wards stop you from doing magic in here too?"

He grinned sheepishly. "Er, no. But I'm not going to materialise in your room. I don't do that. Anymore," he added as an afterthought.

I rolled my eyes. I would have to trust him tonight. "If you do, I'll castrate you."

"Not kill?"

"I don't do that." I gave him a mischievous grin. "Anymore."

He shook his head at me, chortling softly. "Good night then, Léo."

"Night, Raph."

I fled into the room, but I couldn't close the door fast enough to block out his words.

"I've missed you."

Words that could break me. I swallowed thick, pursing my lips before I could admit the same, and slammed the door, left to wonder if they had been intended to be heard.

It was a flimsy barrier, but I felt safer like this. The entire drive I had had to fight the urge to talk to him, to find out what his life had been like these past six years. I was better not knowing. The risk was reconnection and any emotions that would come with that.

We had separated for the good of Étienne, a mutual decision to give our son the best chance at a normal life. I had still loved him then. The feeling had faded over time, but now… Here…

It's just one day, Eléonore. You'll find the bloody bastard tomorrow and part ways with Raph. You can do this.

But…

No excuses. You're a strong, independent woman. You don't need anyone else in your life. Étienne's all that matters.

But…

You can't let Raph back into your life. What would you say to Étienne? What would it do to him?

But…

If this is going to be a problem, you should leave right now.

Oh, shut up.

The duelling voices in my head fell silent. The reasoning side of me made a lot of good points, but it was evading the one thing that was really bothering me.

Raphael and I had gone our separate ways to protect Étienne from unwanted attention. Here I was, though, being hunted and putting my son's life in danger anyway. What did people call that? Ironic bullshit.

Then there was the question that I didn't want to ask, but that was there, in the back of my mind: would I be in this hellhole of trouble if Raphael and I had decided to stay together?

I wanted the answer to be yes, but I was too exhausted to attempt cosmic understanding.

I stayed dressed in my clothes as I fell onto the bed. It was small, but there was too much space. I fell into sleep wishing that Étienne was with me, that I could hold him while I slipped into dreams.

The smell of coffee and fall spices ensnared my senses when I awoke. A quick glance at the clock on the nightstand revealed that the time was a quarter past nine. I shot up and hurried out of the room, stumbling into the kitchen.

"Why did you let me sleep in?"

"Good morning to you too." Raphael glanced up at me from behind a newspaper. His thick curls were even more unkempt than they had been the night before, dark bags underlined his sapphire eyes.

I wondered if I looked as terrible.

He moved to the stove top. "I made a batch of pumpkin spice oatmeal. Care for some?" He held the pot out. "There's also fresh coffee. And I'm stocked up on bacon and eggs. I could fry them in a minute. No trouble at all."

I blinked a few times. "You let me sleep in."

"What was I supposed to do? Materialise in your room and risk castration? Now, I know you're hungry. If nothing's tempting you so far, I can always pop some bread into the toaster. I've got ten different types of jams and peanut butter. I'm not going to let you get away with just coffee. Not with what we have to accomplish."

I shook my head and sank into a chair. This was all too familiar. And comfortable. I couldn't afford to fall into this trap of nostalgia.

"C'mon, Léo. It's just breakfast. You need to eat if you want to kick some ass today."

I nodded a half-hearted agreement. My stomach rumbled too, happy as I considered my options again. I didn't want to accept his cooking, but the smell was too enticing. "Oatmeal, then."

"Excellent. And coffee. Black, right? It's Turkish. Should perk you up. As long as you're not immune yet."

I granted him one chuckle, then glanced at the clock on the wall. It was nine-twenty. Étienne would be sitting in class by now. I wondered if he was thinking of me. Maybe if I focused on him hard enough he would know that I was sending him all my love.

Raphael passed me a mug decorated with St. Joseph's Oratory and slid a bowl of oatmeal across the table.

The wafting scent of autumn billowed up. It smelled too good. The heat of the coffee put my body at ease while wiping away any remnant of sleep. A bite of oatmeal was an explosion of delightful flavours in my mouth. He was still a great cook. I did my best to not let my face reveal the excitement of my taste buds. "Not bad," I offered and took a long sip of coffee to stop me from smiling at his accusatory stare.

"I'm glad it's satisfactory." Reclaiming his seat, he lifted up the paper once more.

I took a chance to shovel another helping into my mouth and barely restrained a sigh of contentment. My tongue darted out of my mouth, licking my lips. The betrayer.

"Just not bad, eh?"

Raphael met my gaze left of the newspaper. He winked then ducked behind it once more as I aimed my spoon at his head.

It stayed in my hand, dropping back into the oatmeal. It would be childish to throw it. Not something I would do at all. But something I would have done.

It was this house, this breakfast. Comfortable and cozy, they plagued my attention. "So where do we find Edmond?"

The paper folded and then got laid aside. "We don't."

Well, that broke the spell of ease. "What?"

"C'mon, Léo. I've known about this bounty for a month. Do you think he'd still be alive if I knew where to find him?"

A tricky question. Raphael was a sorcerer after all. There had to be some code about murdering comrades. Like: don't do it.

"Who are we looking for then?"

"A Novice," Raphael replied slowly. "One of Edmond's. I've been tracking him for two weeks. I'd already planned to ambush him today. Now, I have the pleasure of your company."

Pleasure? I hoped not. "And where do we find him?"

"A pâtisserie."

"A pâtisserie?"

"Oui. He goes there every Tuesday at eleven a.m. for a mint tea and chocolate croissant. Stays for half an hour before making for the Plains of Abraham. He meditates there for an hour, then dematerialises to an unknown location."

"Why haven't you cornered him yet?"

"Because I didn't know until three days ago that he knew Edmond for sure. You think he's the only lead I've been following? C'mon Léo."

"C'mon, Raph!" I threw his words back at him. "Why would I ever think that you've been playing detective for me?"

Raphael frowned. "A lot may have changed in six years. But a lot also hasn't. I haven't stopped caring."

"Well, that makes one of us."

Spiteful and antagonising, the words leaped from my lips. I would have taken them back, but pride stopped me from apologising. The wounded look in his eyes nearly convinced me otherwise, but by the time I considered it a possibility, Raphael stormed out of the kitchen.

I wanted to believe that he had no right to be upset with me. I had hoped for a direct shot at Edmond. The idea of stalking one of Edmond's trainees posed two problems: energy and time. There was a higher chance of failure if we had to use another person for information and there was no chance of this all tying up neatly in a day as I had hoped.

It had taken Raphael a month to get this close. Whatever I held against him, I knew he wasn't incompetent. If it had taken a month, it was because Edmond was that good. If Edmond didn't want to be found, then what was the chance of me pinpointing his location in even half the time Raphael had.

Of course, there was always the option of walking out into the night and proclaiming my presence. I'd prefer to go the less conspicuous route if I could. To do that, though, I would need to make some sort of amends.

Raphael hadn't gotten far. He stood in the bathroom, combing his unruly mop of hair. "I'll be done in a minute," he said without looking at me. "You can take a shower if you want. I've got a body wash, but that's about it."

"That's all I need. Thanks." I hesitated. He was still facing the mirror, refusing to meet my eye. "And I am thankful for your help. I'm just anxious to be done with this, to be back with Étienne. I hadn't realized that you were watching out for me. For us. I… Well, thanks. Really."

Raphael spat a chunk of toothpaste into the sink, then took his time to gargle out his mouth before finally meeting my stare. "I'll get you back home to him, soon as I can." He stepped towards me, then past me.

I should have been glad that he wasn't trying to be chummy with me. But the sudden turn in his demeanour, the firm shut of his door, and the reserved tone of his voice bothered me even more than his friendliness of before.

We walked to the pâtisserie. It was only a few blocks away, and it was a beautiful day. The wind was crisp, but matched with the sun's strength it wasn't that cold at all. Under different circumstances, it would have been the perfect autumn day to visit Mont St-Bruno with Étienne for a hike and to watch the changing leaves. My heart twisted a little, missing him even more as I thought of what we could be doing together if I were anywhere but here with his father.

I had spoken to Rosalie an hour ago to check in. She had given me only good news about Étienne, which eased a bit of my anxiety without completely eradicating it. It had also a prompted a smile of relief from Raphael, his only sign of emotion since he'd assumed his cold front.

In silence, we marched alongside the tourists and residents of Vieux-Quebec. Even with the cooler temperature settling in, street vendors and performers ensnared audiences and patrons. The city was alive and brimming with excitement. I wished I could delight in it with them. Instead, I summoned determination and anger to remind me of what was at stake and what had to be done to guarantee that there would be a day when I could bring Étienne here to experience the history and culture for himself.

Raphael was a quiet companion, tension radiating off him like heat from a fire. Talking strategy seemed the best way to convince him to break it.

"So, what was your strategy? With this Novice? How were you planning on ambushing him?"

"I was going to get him at the Plains. But you're in charge, so it's whatever you want." He sounded even more stiff than before and never once looked my way.

"If your plan is to get him at the Plains, why are we going to the pâtisserie?"

"We can skip to the Plains if you want."

"No, we'll go to the pâtisserie."

"Alright, we'll go the pâtisserie."

I came to an abrupt halt, my hands placed squarely on my hips in the most defiant pose I could muster. Petulant men were worse than their miniature versions. "I'm not going anywhere with you while you're in this mood. We agreed that this isn't about us getting back together, so you don't get to be surly and pissed off because of what I said."

"I'm not surly and pissed off."

"Well, of course not. That big smile on your face is so hard to miss. And then there's that skip in your step. No, not surly and pissed off at all."

It got a smile out of him, but just a small one. "I'm not upset with you," he asserted without any sign of emotion on his face to support his words. "But you were right this morning. You haven't expected anything from me. You have your life now. I have mine. We're doing this for Étienne. Then you can go home to him and get on with your life while I get on with mine."

"That's not what I—" No, that was exactly what I had meant. I just hadn't intended for it to bother him so much. I hadn't expected it to bother me that much either. I had been sure that he would have forgotten about me. I had been sure that he would have been glad to be rid of me. But now it was clear to me that he wasn't putting on this angry face because he was hurt. He was putting it on so he wouldn't get hurt.

I guess we were both the same in that regard. "Can we try to be amicable, at least?"

"Yeah." Finally, a shade of his former self shone through the facade of surliness he had erected. "Toujours des amies."

"Great."

He nodded. "C'mon, Léo. We've got a Novice to find."

Just like that, he was back to being more of his upbeat self. I was half sure that there was even a skip in his step as he led me down the cobbled streets to the pâtisserie.

It was a tiny space, a homely place that exuded warmth. The mellow shades of the walls and the wafting scents of various coffees and desserts were enough to get my mouth salivating. There was limited seating to begin with, and only one table was available when we entered.

We claimed it for ourselves, easing into the plush cushions—the perfect customer trap. Even with the knowledge of what I had to do, the atmosphere enticed me to wish I had hours to spend there, surrounded by a welcoming promise of contentment. But I had no hours to spend, and no contentment to afford to become comfortable in.

"Can I tempt you with a latté? Or maybe a cappuccino?"

"Surprise me."

Raphael winked mischievously and hurried off to the counter.

I took the opportunity to better appraise the clientele that occupied the space. In one corner sat an older couple sharing a slice of what looked to be an apple crumble pie. Near them sat two girls who looked to be about my age. Judging from the maps of Quebec City that they had with them, they were tourists. The German they spoke was the firm proof. Across from them sat a man in his thirties, reading a book I couldn't identify while enjoying what looked to be a piece of maple pie and some sort of hot beverage. Three more tables were occupied, one by a younger couple, and another by a couple my age who were devouring a piece of quiche each. The last held a man of close to my age. He was writing in a journal with only a cup set out before him. The two single men were my only likely choices for the Novice though neither were indulging in the drink or food Raphael had mentioned.

Raphael returned to the table with a plate and two mugs. "He's not here yet," he said as he placed all three on the table.

I was too distracted by the dessert he had brought to respond immediately. On a large plate sat a bundt cake in a pool of amber liquid. Atop it was a dollop of cream decorated with shredded pistachio nuts.

"Is that what I think it is?"

"What do you think it is?"

"I think it's you trying to get me drunk."

"Oh no, you've figured out my master plan." He stuck two forks into the Baba au Rhum. "There's not enough alcohol in here to give us any kind of buzz. Plus, the coffee here is strong. And we're early still. Enjoy yourself a bit."

"This isn't a vacation."

"Then consider it a last meal."

"Jerk." I slugged him one in the arm before I could restrain myself. And then the two of us were laughing and inviting people to stare at us while we did. Sometime during the laughter, I started to cry, and he stopped laughing too.

"C'mon, Léo. Don't cry."

It was only a few tears, but they were too many for me. I took a deep breath and tried to ignore the pang in my heart. I wasn't sure what had brought them on, but I was convinced that missing Étienne was a part of it. The other was for fear that this mission was one that wouldn't be as easy as I had hoped. Perhaps there was another explanation for them too, a tiny one that had to do with regret for the last six years.

"I'm fine," I assured him and took a decent serving of the Baba au Rhum. The cake was wonderfully moist, dense with syrup and rum. I took my time chewing it, trying to stave off any questions. They came anyway.

"While we're waiting, can I ask you about him?"

I kept chewing until there was nothing left in my mouth. With a hard swallow, I released a long breath. "I thought you'd been watching us."

"I've been keeping tabs on you, not stalking you. I've caught glimpses of him," he added warily.

"He's stubborn as his namesake," I said, "And he's got your cheek."

Raphael beamed proudly.

"He just started his first year of school yesterday."

"Wow. Already."

"He's rather precocious."

"Well, with a bookworm for a mother…"

"Thankfully he didn't pick up his father's below average genes."

"And…?" he hesitated to glance quickly around at the other occupants. The elderly couple was shuffling by. He waited for them to pass then whispered almost too low for me to hear, "Magic?"

I shook my head and took another bite of Baba au Rhum.

He understood the message and shovelled a piece into his mouth.

In silence, we waited about ten minutes, finishing off our lattés and dessert, before the Novice finally made an appearance.

He came in at a run and nearly tripped as he did. "Fuck!" he swore as he banged into the man with the maple pie.

"Take it easy, boy," the man warned him then turned abruptly back to his book.

"Sorry, sir," the boy muttered then hurried along to the counter.

"The usual, Gavin?" the woman behind the counter asked.

"Pour apporter, s'il te plaît, Sandrine."

Gavin looked a lot younger than I had expected, and a lot shorter and plumper too. As a Novice he could be as old as two

95

hundred and yet he chose to look like a teenager. As he turned to face away from the counter, I caught a glance of his face through my peripherals. He was even playing up the acne. Either this guy knew how to play below the radar, or he liked to look like the stereotypical teenage outcast, or he was an idiot.

I liked that last option best of all.

Raphael was very stiff in his seat, staring at the empty mug in his hand, his eyes glazed over. I watched him while keeping an eye on Gavin, waiting for him to give me some sign as to what was going to happen next.

He didn't look up and the next moment, the hellhole of trouble we were in expanded into a chasm.

Gavin turned from the counter and glanced in our direction. He saw me as I saw him and I knew that he knew me and that I knew him.

"Fuck!" he swore again and tore out of the pâtisserie.

CHAPTER TWELVE

A Chase

The relationship between Novice and Elder is reminiscent of that between apprentice and master as in Medieval guilds. Most Novices today are not born magical and their tutelage is part intense training and part ridiculing grunge work. Most also have really low self-esteem.

- December 28th 1993

Raphael shot out of his seat. "Well, that was unexpected. C'mon, Léo. The game is afoot."

I bolted after him, ready to give chase. In my haste, I tripped over the chair and stumbled into the table of the man with the book.

He gazed up at me with bemused grey eyes as I issued an apology.

"I just seem to have chosen the wrong place to sit today," he offered graciously and returned his focus to his book. I could see now that it was *The Count of Monte Cristo*.

"Now where?" I demanded as we exited the pâtisserie.

"Our best bet will be to head for the Plains."

"And if he's not there."

"C'mon, Léo. A little positive thinking can take us a long way. The universe reacts to projections. So project that we find him there."

"And if we don't," I pressed firmly.

"I'll blame your negative energy," Raphael warned me then took off before I could strangle him. "I see him!"

I pursued, trusting his eyesight because I couldn't see what he did. We shifted through the crowd, and then I saw what he did: Gavin was a few feet ahead of us, weaving through the throng.

We manoeuvred the best we could, but it was a difficult thing to accomplish as tourists and locals alike blocked our path. Fortunately, Gavin was struggling same as we. With enough persistence, we finally broke through and were hot on his heels.

Gavin spun around and saw the same. His eyes grew round in anger and he leaped off the curb.

I bounded after him.

"Léo, no!"

Hands grasped my arms and roughly pulled me back just as a truck's horn blasted through the air.

A blur of white crossed my vision, but I felt the truck more than saw it as Raphael pulled me into him.

The crowd jostled us, and I caught a few dirty stares cast in our direction. Withering as they were, my sense of discomfort did not come from them, but from the feeling of home I got in Raphael's arms.

He released me before I could shove him aside. Together we looked forward.

Gavin had vanished from sight.

"Merde," I shouted. "Where did he go?"

The stares we drew then were condemning. Two nuns shuffling past us looked ready to exorcise our demons. If only they could.

"You were nearly killed."

I shrugged. Those kind of near death moments were a commonplace occurrence for me. And I was still alive.

"Where did he go?"

"You need to be more careful."

"Thanks, Mom. Next time, I'll look both ways. Now, can we focus on the real problem at hand?"

Raphael frowned at me, but he didn't bother me again with the near collision. "C'mon, Léo."

His hand grasped mine firmly. Before I could pull away, he tugged me forward, forcing us to march at a brisk walk. I struggled at first to keep up with his determined gait, but soon found the energy to match his pace.

"Where are we going?"

"Not far."

Not far was a small park near the cliff edge. It was less busy than the rest of the town. To our right, the Chateau Frontenac, one of Quebec's most stunning edifices, stretched skyward. Grand and majestic, it was a true remnant of the past, a castle rising high above the town with spires and turrets.

"He's not here."

"I know."

"We've lost him for good."

"Always with the glass half empty. Your karma must be something terrible."

"I wouldn't be in this city if it weren't."

"Well let's hope mine can balance us out."

Amusing as the banter was, my nerves were running, my irritation level rising. "Do you have a plan at all? What the hell are—?"

"Kerryn."

"No need to shout."

We revolved on the spot. Behind us stood a teenaged girl. She wore her ebony hair in pigtails, while thick purple-rimmed glasses covered her olive green eyes. Freckles dotted her face.

There was a sweetly strange scent coming from her, like lemons and chocolate, citric enough to convince me she was a demon.

"Raph—"

"We lost the Novice. Can you find him?"

The girl nodded once and giggled. "Oh, Raph. You're always misplacing your things."

I glanced between Raphael and the demon, not sure what to think or feel about the situation.

Grim-faced and unamused, Raphael's gaze bore into the girl's. "Can you find him?"

"Can you introduce us first?"

Her eyes fell on me for the first time, bright with curiosity.

"Eléonore, Kerryn. Kerryn, Eléonore. Content?"

Kerryn's hand shot out. "Pleasure, Eléonore. I've heard all about you."

I stared daggers at her hand, refusing to take it.

She just chuckled and retracted her offer. "No need to be a bitch." She vanished before her last word was spoken. It echoed in the space between Raphael and I.

He wasn't looking at me, his gaze set pointedly at the spot where the demon had just stood.

"You have a demon?"

"Yeah."

"Why the fuck do you have a demon?"

"Can we do this later?" Raphael glowered in my direction. "Please," he added.

I shook my head. "I'm not working with a demon."

"Kerryn's not bad... Not evil."

Not bad. Not evil. Well, that wasn't anything I had ever thought I'd hear from Raphael's lips. We had spent enough years ridding Montreal of the monsters, protecting people from the poison of their curses and intentions. Had he forgotten that? Or had a lot more changed than he was willing to admit?

"Why did you summon her?"

"I didn't—"

"Well, I found the Novice." Kerryn was back, but no longer carefree. A perturbed frown creased her forehead, her lips pursed in dismay.

"And..."

"You're not going to like this."

"Where is he?"

"On the Plains. But he ain't meditating."

I asked before Raphael did, more than a little miffed with her dramatic pauses. "What is he doing?"

"Holding humans hostage."

CHAPTER THIRTEEN

A Loss

Magic is not something sorcerers choose to share with the mundane community. Most of the rules they abide by are meant to at once protect the every day person and then ensure a status quo. Sorcerers stand by an opinion that the best altruistic choices are also self-serving ones.

- January 10th 1994

What was it that people said: the world turned upside down?

At that moment, it seemed like the world had done a whole 360 twice over. My head reeled. My body felt shaken and out of sorts. Innocent people were being threatened, and there could be no doubt that it was for my sake. My enraged emotions were nothing compared to the intense fury that cascaded off Raphael.

"I'm just the messenger, Raph." Kerryn retreated a step and as she did her form wavered. I caught a glimpse of red and gold, but it was too quick to really perceive her true shape.

The swell of Raphael's fury subsided. I breathed deep, only then realizing how much it had affected my own sense of anger. "Sorry, Kerryn." He ran a hand through his curls. There was a wild look of panic in his eye. "How many humans?"

Kerryn twisted one of her pigtails. "Five. Two adults. Two kids. One baby."

"A family?"

Kerryn shrugged. "I guess."

"Merde. Raph—"

"Magic?" Raphael waved me off with a hand, persisting in his interrogation.

"He's got a gun. But he's set up an illusion to keep away other tourists."

"So he's not stupid."

"No, just a bastard with a weapon," I scoffed, manoeuvring around Raphael to plant myself between himself and Kerryn. Who cared if the guy was upholding the law of the Ancients by not using magic to harm innocents? Knowing that a family was imperilled got my blood boiling even hotter. It did not match the heat radiating off Raphael. "I should go alone. I can bargain with him, get him to release them."

"And if he shoots you?"

"He needs me alive."

"There are plenty of places to put a bullet beside the heart," Kerryn mused.

"So let him shoot me." My voice seeped with exasperation; I didn't care for the demon's nonchalant tone, but I wasn't bothered by the idea of being shot either. "Look, I can divert his attention and then you can swoop in and get the family to safety. Worse case scenario, he manages to get me to Edmond. That's all I want anyway. In fact, maybe it would be—"

"No."

"We don't have time to work out a better plan, Raph."

"No."

"Damn you, you promised. I'm in charge. My word is law."

He hesitated, but I could sense his resolve breaking. There was more than just the family at stake at this point.

"She has a point, Raph."

It didn't surprise me that the demon was taking my side on this. Possibly, a highlight of her day would be seeing me taken prisoner by the Novice. Maybe this was all some elaborate trap… Why hadn't I thought of that sooner? I blamed Raphael for that; my trust for him was clouding my judgement.

"It's a nice reward he's offering." My eyes found Kerryn's, accusing.

She laughed, and I cringed. "Think I'm double crossing you?"

"She isn't." Raphael clutched my arm and spun me to face him. "She can't."

"How can you be—"

"Just trust me."

If time wasn't pressing, I would have fought. I told myself that was the truth, because admitting that it was easy to accept Raphael's word made me feel weak.

"Fine, but then we do it my way."

"Okay." His hand found mine, and he squeezed it tenderly. "Be careful."

"Careful is my middle name."

"Is that before or after Alma?"

I didn't want to smile, not while a family's life was in danger because of me, but I couldn't help it. "This isn't really the time for that."

He stepped back and glanced past me. "Don't bring her immediately into view."

His eyes settled on me one last time. "Just keep him occupied and Kerryn will take care of the rest."

My protestations went unheard as the demon's hand fell over my wrist and our surroundings vanished.

Everything went dark for a second and then I found myself standing on the Plains. Tourists were milling about, nonplussed by our sudden appearance. With a quick glance, I knew where Gavin was. I couldn't see him but the people moving across the Plains were doing their best to avoid a spot a few feet from where we stood.

"His back's to you. Walk forward."

I glanced to my left, where the voice had come from, but there was nothing to see there.

Despite the voice in my head warning me to ignore Kerryn's instructions, I trudged ahead, doing my best to keep my anxiety at bay. I hadn't admitted it to Raphael because I hated to know just how nervous I was. My fears were plenty for the family in danger, but there was also an excitement rushing through me, a hope that Gavin would take me to his master before Raphael or Kerryn could interfere.

A spark of energy ran through me, and I faltered on the spot, spinning around. I saw them then, the family huddled together, held at gunpoint. Even with the distance between us, I could see them shivering. They were a young family, the parents somewhere in their early forties, the oldest child no more than ten.

Gavin smirked at me, the barrel of his gun moving away from the family, targeting my person instead. Just as expected.

Kerryn was nowhere in sight, but I knew she was there with me, walking beside me, ready to strike.

"Mademoiselle Dormant." He took a step forward. "Glad you could join us."

Tourists continued to meander around the hidden circle that Gavin had created for himself. The magic he was channelling was powerful, and every few seconds I felt a wave of it push against

105

me. The energy it required to keep it up didn't seem to be taking a toll on him yet, but with enough time he would falter and so would it. And then things would really get out of hand.

"You can let them go now."

He laughed and his gun found the father's head. The man stared up at it, stoic. I could see the panic behind his calm exterior. He was only a few years older than my father had been when he had died for me. "A good warrior doesn't toss away his shield."

"A good warrior doesn't cower behind innocents. If you want to do battle…" I drew Éponine and stepped forward. "Let's do battle."

The laugh died on his lips, and he cocked the trigger. "Drop it."

I obeyed because there was nothing I could do. With five people at his disposal, I wasn't about to question Gavin's willingness to off one to make a point.

"Now," he said slowly, "where's Raphael?"

His question caught me off-guard, and I fumbled to give an answer. "He's not… I don't… I'm here alone."

"Liar," he hissed, his gun pressing firmly into the man's forehead.

"I'm not—"

"I'm here." Raphael materialised out of thin air, appearing between myself and Gavin.

I stared daggers at his back. How long had he been hiding there, invisible to my eye?

"What now, Novice?"

"I could pull the trigger."

My hands curled into fists; my fury compelled both by Gavin's threats and Raphael's subterfuge. If he had been there all along, he had some sort of plan. I despised not being privy to his intentions. As far as I could see, there were three options open to me:

One. Let Raphael take charge and let his plans unfold as they were, whatever they might be.

Two. Damn Raphael and his plan and offer myself as a willing sacrifice to Gavin so that he would take me to Edmond and deal with the consequences of that after the fact.

Three. Use my words to convince the earth to come to my aid and hope that it answered as it had the night before.

I hated that all three left me vulnerable to chance. The need to fight Gavin was a palpable force. If I could have wielded that darkness in me, I could have decimated him right there and then. I wished I could.

Stay calm. Careful. Kerryn's voice was in my head, offering a reassurance that also sent chills through me. *Trust Raph.*

I bristled with contempt; demons didn't order me about.

"Let them go," Raphael said in a voice that was too calm. "No one needs to get hurt."

"You're right," Gavin agreed, his stance not wavering. "We can all walk away unscathed. But that will require Mademoiselle Dormant to come with me. Quietly."

"No problem," I concurred.

Raphael and Gavin both turned towards me. In that instant, a third variable came into play, one I hadn't foreseen.

The father leaped up, wrestling to get the gun out of Gavin's hands. His wife screamed as he did, his daughters crying out in dismay while the baby wailed.

Magic rolled off Gavin. It all happened too quickly for any of us to react. His left hand swung down, and a pulse surged from his palm, colliding with the father's chest.

The man flew back and landed on the ground in a dead heap.

I darted forward.

Gavin cocked the gun and aimed it at the youngest girl who began to sob uncontrollably. The mother shifted, using her body to shield her daughter from the threat of a bullet.

I pulled short, my knees going weak. *Mother Mary, don't let him shoot.*

"If you shoot them, I will kill you." Behind the steady timbre of Raphael's voice wavered a deep contempt. I could sense it from where I stood. I suspected Gavin did too as he flinched, his manic expression slipping.

"No one else has to get hurt. Mademoiselle Dormant." Gavin's eyes were round and demanding. There was no bluff. If there was no compliance, he would kill each and every one of the remaining family members.

I lifted my arms and stepped forward. Five long strides and I came par with Raphael.

He glanced at me, his expression plain. No fear. Resolved. There was a plan brewing in his mind, but I didn't want him to save me. This was my best chance of getting to Edmond. "Just protect them," I muttered so that only he could hear. "Don't worry about me."

Silence met my request.

"Mademoiselle Dormant."

Seven more steps and I was a foot away from Gavin, my eyes stuck on the gun and the wife it was trained on. Her eyes were locked on mine, conveying confusion, fear, and the smallest glint of hope.

Mother Mary, protect them, I implored one more time.

"You can stop there."

Gavin's tone bristled with malice, but I was beyond obedience at this point.

I hesitated for the briefest moment to create the illusion of compliance, then I hurled myself at him, my hand reaching for the gun.

Caught unawares, Gavin did not fire at once but turned the gun towards me. Then he pulled the trigger.

And missed.

I crashed into him. We struggled for control of the gun. He held tight to it, refusing to relinquish it to me.

We wrestled on the ground in desperation before Gavin remembered that he was a sorcerer and projected me backward with a thought.

I hit the ground, dazed and looked up just as the gun targeted the family again.

"Don't!" I yelled. Too late.

He pulled the trigger and the sound of the shot echoed through my heart. The bullet did not find the mother's head despite the barrel being pointed at her head.

It struck Gavin instead, the bullet ripping through his chest.

The mother bent over her daughters, shielding their bodies as blood splattered them like rain falling from the sky.

I felt conflicted, part of me rejoicing to see the injury done to him. A greater part of me frustrated that my strongest lead to Edmond was bleeding out on the grass.

109

I dashed towards him, but he vanished, leaving only a trail of blood to mark the place where he had just lain.

I whirled around. Raphael had disappeared too.

Screams filled the air around me, people now able to see what they had been previously blocked from. My gaze went with theirs to where the woman shook her husband's prone form, shouting his name over and over again: "Philippe!"

It took her another five minutes of desperate pleading to realise what I already had.

He was dead.

CHAPTER FOURTEEN

A Release

Elders are like the middle child of sorcerers. Petulant. Needy. Always hoping to forge their own path and never caring about whose life they might ruin along the way. I've known some good ones and some rather devious ones in my time. One in particular has become my closest friend. And he is the one I will trust my daughter to when I'm gone.

- December 20th 1993

I stuck around only long enough to see aid come for the woman, before rushing off. Raphael had abandoned me, but I wouldn't let him keep me in the dark.

After shouting his name a few times and then Kerryn's without any answer, I finally got the message: they didn't want to be found.

Why were there never a pack of demons around when you needed them?

If I couldn't release this frustration through hunting, there was always a more positive alternative.

I found a quiet spot in the park where Kerryn had first approached us. The clock on my phone showed three-thirty. School had let out, but Étienne might not be with Rosalie yet. I took the chance anyway. And was rewarded for it.

"Maman?"

"Mon p'tit prince." To hear his voice was like taking a drink of water after struggling through the desert for years. "How are you?"

"Okay. I miss you."

"I'm missing you terribly too."

"Will you be coming home soon?"

"Soon," I promised. *Don't let that be a lie, Mary.*

"When?"

"A few more days. Not long. You'll see. By the time I'm back you'll be wishing me gone again." I would be satisfied if that last line didn't come to pass. "Now tell me about your day."

He did, rambling on first about Mr. Laurier. The he spoke about how only one other girl in the class besides himself could multiply all the way to one hundred with the ten times table. Nathalie had also, he told me, read the entire bibliographical works of Mr. Roald Dahl. I was ready for him to tell me that she was telepathic and was glad when that revelation never came.

"It she pretty?"

"Not like you, Maman."

Words a mother lived to hear. It had been a wise decision to call him; it brought me such ease to hear his voice, to know that he loved me. We talked on until Rosalie insisted that the radio waves from her cell phone weren't good for Étienne's health.

"I'll call you again tonight before bed, okay? Be careful and do everything Aunt Sally says."

"Oui, Maman."

"Je t'aime, mon p'tit prince."

"I love you too."

Our short chat, all forty-five minutes of it, had diminished my rage. In its place, my heart was weighed down with homesickness and a growing dread that I might never see my son again. I needed to move, to walk, to do something. *Find Edmond.*

That was my purpose for being here. Raphael be damned; I could get out of this hellhole of trouble on my own.

"Been looking for you."

Kerryn appeared behind me, flipping her pigtails with a darkly pleased grin.

"Where's Raphael? And the bloody Novice?"

"Bloody indeed, and dealt with. You should have heard him scream." The sadistic grin on her face widened. She extended a hand "Come with me."

My hands balled into tight fists at my sides, refusing to take hers. "Where?"

"To Raph."

"I'm not going anywhere with you."

Kerryn shrugged. "I don't care one way or the other. Raph sent me, but he knew you probably wouldn't like it. So you can just meet him at the apartment." She tossed me a key.

I caught it without losing hold of her gaze. Staring hard enough, I could see the demonic glint, the shadow of her true self lurking close to the surface. I focused on it, and felt from her a strength I had never perceived in any before.

"What's your story, then?"

The humanistic facade almost slipped, the pleasure of Kerryn's expression twisting it to near malice. I stepped back, repelled by it.

"I have many stories," she said in a low voice, the kind that people used to warn off others. Somehow, her way of saying it made me believe that she was contemplating how to kill me. "Don't be vague, Léo."

"Don't call me that." To hear my pet name slip off her tongue made my blood boil. The irritation replaced my fear.

113

She laughed, a titter that would befit most teenagers, complete with condescension and taunting. "You humans and your jealousy."

"I am *not* jealous of you."

"Not even a little? Don't tell me you don't wonder if he took me to bed."

The mental image came to mind before I could fight it away. I swallowed the thick wad of bile that crawled up my throat. "Even if he did"—and I seriously doubted that he had—"I don't care."

"Drawing your sword would probably attract unwanted attention."

Her words led me to realize that my hand was resting on Éponine's hilt. Unconsciously, my fist had curled around it, prepared to decapitate the demon.

"Maybe you should tell your hand to care a little less." She laughed again, and I could clearly detect the deep and grating sound of the demonic creature she was concealing.

The bile rose in my throat again; I had to swallow harder than before to get it to stay down.

With a wink, she skipped away into the dark shadows of a great tree and melted into them.

I unclenched my other fist and saw the key that lay there. Beneath it, the palm of my hand was marked with the exact same shape.

Maybe both my hands could do with a lesson in apathy.

The apartment was empty.

I wasted hours waiting for Raphael to return. I read a little, then tried to do a little research on my phone. I quickly found an article that made mention of the death of a man on the Plains. They claimed he had suffered a heart attack. The words hostage and gunman were missing from the report.

I flung my phone at the cushion opposite me on the couch, then threw the remote control across the room. It crashed into the dining table, and the batteries flew out.

"Raphael!"

It was the the fourth time I had tried calling him and the fourth time he ignored me.

Like a fool, I continued to wait for him to get back. My hands itched for action, my body was tense and needed to release the energy pent up within it. I craved hunting as a junkie longs for that next rush of drugs coursing through his veins.

At one point my stomach began to growl, and I made a mess of his cupboards and fridge to prepare myself a much needed peanut butter and blueberry jam sandwich. I washed it down with a large cup of black coffee. It had been the wrong decision; full of energy and caffeine, my need to hunt was stronger than ever.

I couldn't wait anymore. I threw on my dark jeans and a black hoodie and made for the door.

Would you believe that the handle jingled just as I reached for it? Well, it did.

I brandished Éponine at the entrance, though there was no chance that it could be anyone but Raphael.

He ambled in, head down, stopping only when Éponine's tip burrowed into his chest.

"Ow," he muttered and looked up.

I stepped back. There was a bit of blood dripping from the blade. I smiled at the sight.

There were dark bags under his eyes that hadn't been there before. His motions were lethargic, his index lazily fingering the wound. His eyes wearily appraised the blood that marked it.

"Lovely to see you too," he muttered and sucked his finger to remove the offending stain.

I sheathed Éponine. Any pity I would have felt for his obviously drained appearance fell away as I remembered the day's events, all the lies he had told, and the life it had cost us.

"I've been calling for you."

"Can I eat before we get into this?" He shambled past me.

I pursued him into the kitchen and planted myself between him and the fridge.

His eyes roved the messy counters, and the heaviest of sighs wracked his body. "C'mon, Léo."

"C'mon. C'mon. C'mon," I spat vehemently into his face. Then, I slapped him.

His head jerked under the force. His tired body stiffened. Even in his eyes, I could see a glint of emotion breaking through the dimness.

"You left me on the Plains. A man is dead because of us, and they're saying it's a heart attack. Does his family remember anything? Three children are fatherless now. A woman is widowed. And you left me on the Plains? Where's Gavin now? Is he dead? Did you kill him? Did you question him first? Did you get any answers from him? Why did you leave me on the Plains? And then to send that demon to fetch me. Why her? And why do you have a demon working with you, anyway? Have you slept with her—No, don't answer that question. That doesn't matter."

"What question do you want me to answer?"

His placating tone goaded me to action.

I lunged at him. My fists pummelled his torso with punches—it was the only part of his body that they could reach.

He didn't try to stop me, and it would have been so easy for him to restrain me if he had. He accepted my assault wordlessly, like a martyr. His stoicism built the fire of my rage. I might have stopped earlier if he had actually shown some anger in his expression or the smallest degree of regret. I wanted him to feel like I did. I wanted to see that he was breaking inside too.

I faltered before he could, exhausted by the effort. My hands ached from the toilsome action of repeatedly bashing him. I stepped away from him, panting heavily.

Raphael stumbled back too, gripping the edges of the counter. I was glad to see that his chest was heaving a bit. A crack of something that looked like regret shone in his eyes. It was a good start.

"I'm sorry, Léo. I tried so hard to not..." His body wavered. He reached for a chair and sank into it. "I haven't lost anyone since..."

Since my father. That was one commonality we shared.

His fist fell into the table, and a crack marred the wood surface. The energy of it was strong enough to crash into me, and I fell back into the fridge, shocked by the rage that contorted his features.

I had wanted his anger, but the fury that he emanated menaced me, almost too powerful to behold.

"I couldn't take you with me. It wasn't for you to deal with. I was the one who had tracked the Novice. I was the one who hadn't been careful enough. He recognized you, but he knew me too. That shouldn't have been the case. The man that died... The father... He died because of me, Léo."

117

"It wasn't—"

"It was!" There was a darkness billowing in his eyes that scared me even more than his anger.

"What did you do to Gavin?"

"Do you really want to know?"

I really didn't, but... "Yes."

He rose up from the chair and sauntered towards me. I stayed frozen against the fridge, held in part by my own compulsion to know and by the magic of his will.

"I broke him. Over and over again. I carved him like he was a piece of marble and I some Michelangelo. I brought him close to death, then gave him back life. I poured my energy into him when his failed so that he could suffer every possible moment. I stopped only when continuing threatened to kill us both. And then I eviscerated him while he was still alive and able to cry."

Raphael recounted the details in a grave voice that held no repulsion, nor pleasure. When he was done, he towered over me, his body curving towards me.

"I couldn't let you see that," he whispered with sudden tenderness and ran a hand through my hair.

My knees quivered. Angry though I was, I could not hate him after hearing what he had done. He'd nearly killed himself to ensure the Novice suffered the most pain possible. He deserved praise for that. He deserved...

"I would have helped you," I told him. "I would have given you some of my life. To make it last longer."

"You have given more than enough in sufferance already. It was the least I could offer."

He took a step back from me, but I could still feel the heat of his proximity. Not only on my skin. Within my body.

My mind and my heart were in a battle, but it was pure instinct that triumphed both.

With a cry, I leaped at him, my hands scrambling towards his shoulders, pushing me up so that my lips could collide with his.

He stiffened at first, taken aback by the swiftness of my action. It did not take him long to accept me.

His hands curved around my body, supporting me. He pressed me into the fridge, our mouths moving together, our passions colliding, stripping away all our reason, all our logic. We were prisoners to our desires and our frustrations, and we were neither of us strong enough to fight it.

So we succumbed and our lovemaking endured.

We came together three times. Each time we grew more feral, our passion rising not falling. The last time, he lost control of his magic, and I felt it wash over me, felt all his need and desire, all his want. I knew how much he wanted to possess me, to hold me, to satisfy me, to make me happy. The swell of it drove me to Nirvana and beyond. My body burned with the greatest fire it had ever known, greater even than the night when Étienne had been conceived.

I collapsed upon him, our naked bodies entwined upon his bed. His arms held me close to him. We were both crying, both struggling to breathe, both ensnared by bliss.

The feeling would be gone when the morning came. We would both regret relinquishing to our decision and wish we had exercised more caution.

For the moment, we fell asleep, still together, entirely at peace.

CHAPTER FIFTEEN
A Meeting

I faced my first demon when I was ten. My father brought it home after a night of hunting and chained it up in the basement just for me. It took a week for me to find the courage to face it. And then fifteen stabs before I finally decimated her.

- November 6th 1993

I woke first to the streaming sunlight. It fell over us, illuminating the error of the night before. Wondrous as it had been, it had eased me of the tension and anger that I had borne these past few days.

I also had never felt so terrible, wracked with a guilt that churned my stomach.

I slid away from Raphael. He stirred but did not wake. As silently as possible, I crept around the room, scrambling to retrieve the pieces of clothing that had been unceremoniously strewn across his bedroom floor. My hoodie was ripped down the front. My bra was in no better shape, lying in two separate pieces. That man had been rather impatient. I smiled a little at the memory, then trembled in disgust.

What had I done?

I saw my phone next and remembered Étienne. I had forgotten to call him last night.

One glance showed that I had three messages and six missed calls.

Still naked, I fled into the hall and chanced a call. It was seven o'clock. School only started at eight-thirty. Plenty of time.

Rosalie answered halfway through the first ring.

"You're an idiot."

"I know. My phone was on silent all night."

"And what were you doing?"

"What do you think?" It wasn't exactly a lie.

"You told him you'd call. Couldn't you have taken a moment to phone him while you were doing it." I couldn't imagine what her reply would be if she knew the whole truth.

"I'm calling now. Can I talk to him?"

"He's getting ready for school..."

"Sally!"

"I'll see if he wants to talk, okay? That's the best I can do."

"Thanks." I threw a final glimpse behind me. Raphael still hadn't emerged. It was cold in his apartment. I really should have put on some clothes first.

"Hello." The aloofness of Étienne's voice kicked me in the gut.

"Bonjour, mon p'tit prince. I'm so—"

"I'm getting ready for school. Can we talk later?"

I swallowed down the sour taste of his resentment. "I love you, Étienne."

"Bye, Maman." I heard him call for Aunt Sally.

"Ellie?"

"I'll call back this afternoon."

"Ellie..."

"Bye."

I hung up before her pity could affect me too.

121

"Léo."

Raphael emerged from the bedroom wearing pants. I was cruelly aware of my bare flesh in comparison. He did not look down, his eyes holding mine. It was a kindness on some level, but it opened that vulnerable part of me to his scrutiny.

I hurried past him into the guest room to change, slamming the door shut.

"Léo," he called again from the other side of the door.

"I'm leaving," I told him. "Last night wasn't supposed to happen. It was part of the rules."

"Where will you go?"

"That's not your concern."

"Stay, Léo. What happened last night won't happen again."

I couldn't trust his word on that. Because I couldn't trust myself. If self-control wasn't in the realm of possibility, the next course of action was avoiding the temptation completely.

"C'mon, Léo. I know we hit a dead end with the Novice, but together—"

I shoved the door open, and Raphael jumped back a foot to avoid getting hit. "I'm doing the rest of this alone."

"Why are you being like this?"

He reached for me, but I evaded him, retreating towards the door. "Because I need to be my best self for my son and I can't do that with you here. If you care about Étienne as you say you do, you'll let that be enough."

He shook his head at me, but silently gestured for me to go. "If you need me…"

"I won't need you," I told him flatly and hurried out of the apartment before he could find any other words to convince me otherwise.

The questions of where I would stay and how I would go about finding Edmond didn't worry me. Out in the crisp autumn air, I felt like I could breathe again. Last night, though a bad decision, had helped to soothe a lot of my inner demons. My head was clearer, and I would take my time to find a way to the sorcerer and put an end to the bounty on my head.

Setting off, I shoved my hands into my pockets. It was a surprise to feel a paper in the left one. I would have ripped it in two without looking at it, but some part of me was curious enough to see what Raphael had written.

Except, it wasn't from Raph.

I read the words once, then again, sure that I was just imagining the message. The fourth time assured me that it was real. I read it a fifth time anyway.

Chère Mademoiselle Dormant,

It would be my greatest pleasure if you would join me tomorrow, that is September 5th, at the pâtisserie. I will be there most of the morning. If you decide to come, I ask only one thing: that you do not bring your friend.

If you do not come, I will assume that you do not wish to bring this amicably to an end.

If you do not come, you will not see your son again. Is that an ample threat? I imagine it is.

Tomorrow then. At noon latest.

Bonne santé,

Edmond Cartier

I ripped up the paper until the pieces that lay in my palm were too small to reduce anymore. When I was done, I threw them into the air. They were carried away by the gusting wind.

It was hard to place my emotions. There was an excitement to know that there would be no need to waste hours searching for the man. But there was also frustration, the most I'd felt since discovering the hellhole of trouble that was threatening to swallow me.

No one, no fucking one, would threaten my son and live to tell about it.

It was early in the morning, but the pâtisserie was busier than it had been the day before. Though fewer tables were occupied, there were more people placing orders at the counter.

I recognized the maple pie man and the doting elderly couple. The only other customer was a doctor in scrubs. She was slowly devouring a croissant that was stuffed with a fried egg and oozing with cheese. My stomach churned a little, remembering that it was hungry.

Deal with it, my mind insisted.

"Bonne journée, Mademoiselle Dormant. I was hoping you would come."

I revolved on the spot.

The man with the maple pie smiled warmly up at me.

"Care to join me?"

"Edmond."

"Oui." He rose and extended a hand.

I stayed my distance, unable to come to terms with the idea that this guy was an Elder and the damned sorcerer responsible for the bounty on my head. I had bumped into him yesterday. He could have taken me then.

Instead, he had slid a note into my jacket pocket.

This was a dangerous man.

But I was a dangerous woman. I sat in the chair opposite him and leaned back. I took the time to better appraise his appearance. He was clean-shaven, his dark brown hair parted down the middle. Not a single strand fell in his face. His clothes had the neat and ordered look to it too.

He smirked and took his seat too. "You should take my hand." He offered it again.

"You shouldn't have threatened my son."

"You killed my Novice."

"I doubt you really care."

He chortled and took another bite of pie. "True."

The stench of his arrogance was deplorable, but it was his easy attitude that set me most on edge. He was unperturbed by the whole ordeal. "So what now?"

"Why don't you order yourself something. I personally adore the maple pie, but I hear the chocolate croissants are out of this world. Some would even say they're to die for."

His laughter was even worse, a careless display. The more he conveyed a nonchalance towards the lives wasted for his gain, the more I trembled with the realisation that I was in way over my head.

"I'm not really hungry," I told him curtly.

"A drink, then. The chai latte is divine." He raised his mug and tilted it towards me, in offer of some toast. Whether to my health or to my death I couldn't be certain. "My treat."

125

"No. That's okay." I tried to be civil, thinking—more like hoping—it would keep the status quo.

"Well, all I can do is offer." He grinned and took another bite of pie. "I suppose it's straight to business then. Tell me, will this be one of those hard talks, or can we make this amicable?"

"Depends on what you want from me. And what you plan to do to my son."

"What I plan to do to Étienne depends on how this goes." Edmond leaned back in his seat, his fingers drumming against the table.

I bristled at the sound of my son's name leaving his lips. "So tell me what you want from me?"

"First, tell me why you came here?"

"You invited me."

"No," he laughed, like some teacher condescending a child who just asked a stupid question. "Tell me why you came to the city."

I shrugged. "I heard that there was a bounty on my head in the six digits. I figured it was too good of an opportunity to pass up on."

When he laughed this time, I could detect in it, and in his face, the growing signs of annoyance. "Why did you really come?" he asked me again. His eyes narrowed, his teeth glinted beneath his smiling lips.

I gave him the honesty he wanted. "To kill you."

He clapped his hands together. "Oh ho! Yes! To kill me. I thought that was it. I'm so glad it is."

The more I saw of the sociopath that he was, the more I wished I had thought through a better plan than just appearing here like a dog called by its master. If the chance came, I would kill him here, in front of all these people, and deal with the consequences after. But only once I had guaranteed Étienne's safety. That was what I needed from him.

"And how did you plan to kill me?" It was hard to accept how genuine his curiosity was.

He was really getting under my skin now. If he had just put out this damned bounty for a chance to meet me... "Look, I don't know what you want from me. I came to kill you, whether that meant blowing the brains out of the back of your head or slitting your throat. But if I can get you to promise to drop the bounty off and call off the greedy demons that keep coming for me, then I'll let you live."

"And what do I get in return?"

"Besides your life?"

"If we were to imagine that there was any realm of possibility in which you would be able to kill me."

"I still don't know what you wanted from me in the first place."

"Don't you?"

"No." I rose. "And I'm tired of talking. If you won't leave my son alone, then know that I will kill you." I was aware that I was drawing stares. A hush had filled the pâtisserie. I ignored it. "Not now. But soon."

"And you imagine my death will solve your problems?"

"Yeah, I do."

He shook his head, sombre. "You are very naive, Mademoiselle Dormant." He removed a phone from his pocket and slid it towards me. It was open on a video.

The room around me was moving again, people chattering to fill the silence. I saw nothing of them, my eyes fixated on the small screen and the scene playing out upon it.

There was my son, my Étienne, sitting in the schoolyard, reading a book.

The breath left me, and I reeled on the spot. My hand reached for the chair to steady myself. The lightheartedness that captured me brought with it a dizzying sensation. Then through the shock of the plain threat, a new fury bubbled through me. It brought with it clarity and a sharpening of my senses. I felt the fire bursting in my gut. If it had been in my power, I could have burned down the entire pâtisserie with it.

"You fucking bastard!" I took the phone and threw it at him.

Edmond caught it deftly in his hand, his movements fluid and agile. He stared at the screen for a moment.

"Excuse me." The elderly man approached us. "Is everything good?" he asked in a compassionate tone, his French accent prevalent. "I may help you."

"Non. Merci," I shooed him away with a brief smile of gratitude.

He smiled too, skeptical, but ultimately retreated back to his worrying wife.

"Fuck you," I said again, lowering my voice this time.

"Please, Mademoiselle Dormant, there's no need for that. No harm will come to dear Étienne if you comply."

"With what?"

Edmond took the last piece of his pie and chewed it. It was excruciating to watch him milk it, a façade of savouring. He rose then. "You will meet me tonight. Alone. At the Citadelle. There we will discuss what it is I want from you."

"Why can't we discuss it now?"

"That is not my wish."

"Then why meet me here in the first place?"

"For just that. To meet. And so you could understand."

"What am I supposed to have understood?"

He laughed again, the belittlement in his voice darkened by malice. "That you are not in control."

He nodded and the world went still.

I blinked, and he was gone.

The hellhole of trouble had finally swallowed me whole.

CHAPTER SIXTEEN

A Visit

*The first demon hunter was a sorcerer. In the thirteenth century,
a feudal lord, Rialle, discovered a crack between planes. After decimating
the demonic straggler, he sewed the gap shut. With passing time, more
cracks appeared and sorcerers did their best to heal each and every one and
eradicate the satanic spawn. Seven hundred years later, we're still
struggling with the illegal aliens.*

- January 3rd 1995

What would you have done in my place?

He wanted me to come tonight. There was every chance
that he would kill me, or at the very least torture me. But he had
threatened my son.

What would you have done?

I had seen enough movies, read enough books, to know
that this wasn't going to go my way. But what choice had he left me
with? My life or my son's. That made my decision an easy one.

Really easy.

Hopping in Marianne, I drove away from Quebec City,
away from any chance of bumping into Raphael. It was what I
needed to do for myself. To find a place where I could breathe and
appreciate things I hadn't before. In case this night happened to be
my last.

Was I supposed to think anything else, to believe that I
hadn't already seen my last dawn, that I would never lay my eyes on
my son again?

It was that last thought that really drove me out of town. I would have taken the road right back to Montreal, but I was afraid of endangering his life. So I drove to the only place I knew I could find the silence I needed to just sit and reflect.

The Montmorency Falls. It was my father who had first taken me there. My first memory of it was as a girl of five. The cascading water hadn't scared me at all. I had been shaken to stand in its presence because its might had been too strong to not be moved by it. But the sensation had empowered me, not intimidated me. I had felt the tremendous possibility of the world at that moment, and I would not forget it. The world was big and could be terrifying; if I wanted to survive it, I had to be bigger, braver. I think that might have been the lesson my Dad had wanted me to learn. He had never told me. I had never asked.

I continued coming to our old haunt, even after his passing, to find solace in the might of the falls, to abide in the memories I had of our time together. It was one of the places where I could feel the ghost of him.

It was that connection that I needed to bring me some comfort.

The parking lot was fairly empty; no surprises there, it was a school day after all.

I followed my well-known path into what was now a popular tourist spot. From afar, I watched people mingling on the bridge that hung over the waterfall. They took pictures, admiring nature's terrible and fierce beauty from a safe distance. Most of them were content to be there, relatively secure. Most would never seek to abandon protocol and forge their own path.

I could never be like them.

My path was the treacherous one, following the unmarked trail my father had shown me all those years. Through the untamed flora, I made my way, approaching the wonder of nature that stood roaring. It stood the test of time. It watched people come and go, it had seen faces grow, it had seen people disappear. It had known loss, maybe not felt it, but there were stories woven into it.

Damn, I was getting too philosophical with all these thoughts.

I shrugged them away and focused on the final obstacle of my journey. Grasping the cliff face, I began the descent towards a jutting rock. It was not an easy task, the rocks slippery from the waterfall's mist. Nothing a little wariness couldn't overcome.

The ledge was a little wet, but I sat upon it without any reservations and stared at the water that sped past me, a constant and ferocious movement that swept away the land beneath it. I almost wished to throw myself into it and let it carry me where it would, wherever that might be.

Unfortunately, I wasn't one to believe in suicide. If I had to die, it would have to be at the hands of another. And I would have to take them with me.

I sat for hours, the sun moving across the sky, towards the day's end. Most I spent in rumination, some in silence, some speaking aloud words that I wanted my father to hear, words I wished he could respond to.

"I wanted to live a bit longer than this. You made it to what, thirty-six? I was hoping for that at least. I guess that's just another decision that's out of our hands. At least I had a kid. That's something. A legacy, right? But he might be lucky enough to miss all this. I tried to keep it separate, family and work, but I know that you wouldn't approve of that. You would approve of Étienne, though. He's proving worthy of his namesake."

I rambled on like that for a while, my voice breaking every so often. It cracked when I thought too much of how the two Étienne's in my life would never meet.

Then I spoke of dying. "Were you afraid of the end, Dad? That night when you threw yourself in the path of that attack meant to kill me. It was sudden, but you acted so quickly. Had you always been ready to die for me? I get it, you know. I'm ready to die tonight if only it can guarantee Étienne's safety. Did you know that mine was guaranteed when you did? Or were you only giving me my best shot? If Raphael hadn't come that night... Well, I won't depend on him again. Maybe you think I should. But I can't. I can't trust Étienne with him. His best chance of a normal life is with Sally."

Luckily, my will already stipulated that Étienne was to be entrusted to Rosalie's care in the event of my death.

I spoke a bit longer, telling him about my job, telling him about Étienne. It had been three years since I had last come here. I wanted to believe that he was somehow aware of everything that had happened in that time. Not that I believed in paradise or a heaven, but you didn't spend most of your life hunting demons and not believing that there was some spiritual world beyond the one we knew.

"Maybe I'll be seeing you soon, Dad. Maybe I'll be seeing Mom too."

My wallet was in my hand without a thought, my fingers reaching into a sleeve to pull out a worn and sepia-toned photograph. It was crinkled with age and use. The image was one I

133

knew well, but I stared at it with no less intent than I had the first time.

My mother and father stared up at me, grinning in the shade of the willow tree that had once stood on my paternal grandparents' property. They were in their late teens, and my mother was visibly pregnant with me. She wore a flowing dress with a Celtic cross dangling from her neck—an homage to her Irish heritage. Despite the image's colouring, it was evident that her hair was a flaming red, bound in a messy bun. Some of it fell over her face. My dad was in the process of brushing them aside for her, one strand already wound about a finger.

Bliss exuded from them. I tried to embrace it in my heart, but all the photograph managed to bring me was regret that I'd never had the opportunity to know my mom. She had passed away a few months after this picture was taken, only a few weeks after I was born. My dad had always said that she had taken sick because of a weak immune system. She hadn't died giving birth to me, but it was my birth that had killed her. My father hadn't let me feel guilt over that, and I didn't. Though I didn't blame myself for what had happened, I still was able to feel remorse for the time we had lost out on.

Time was as unkind as ever. I could waste no more in this place. I kissed the photograph once and swallowed down the emotions rising up. I gave my surroundings one final look. Chances were, I wasn't ever coming back.

"Until next time, Dad. Might not be so long now."

The sun was already setting, and I risked traffic getting back into the city. I should have left earlier, but what was done was done. I had wanted to stay, and so I had. There were still some things to take care of before I could leave.

I waited until I was in the car before I made the few calls that had to be made.

The first was to Catherine.

"Atwater Library. How may I help you?"

"Hi, Cathy."

"Oh lord, Eléonore! It's good to hear your voice. I've been so worried about you. You left so quickly…"

"I know. I'm sorry about that."

"Don't give it a second thought. I have Ferdinand covering your shift. He has no spine, that lad. It's so easy to make him do my bidding. Say hi, Ferdinand."

I heard a low male voice rumble a greeting. It brought a needed smile to my face. Catherine's attitude was infectious.

"Hey, Ferdinand. It's a wonder he hasn't run away from you."

"He's too afraid of what I'll do when I catch him… Guess he's not as stupid as he looks."

She got me to laugh, a real moment of amusement. I relished in it, but it was gone too soon.

"You coming home soon, dear?"

"Soon as I can," I lied. I wondered then how many more times I would have to make the false promise to people I cared for. To people who cared about me.

"I know that Rosalie is watching out for Étienne, but if there's anything I can do…"

"You're too sweet, Cathy. But there's nothing really. I'll see you in a few days."

"You look after yourself, you hear?"

135

"Aye, aye, captain."

"And Eléonore…" Her voice caught me just in time, my finger poised on the red button. "Stay away from those French boys. They'll break your heart."

Catherine had been the easy call, just a friend I felt obliged to say goodbye to one last time.

The next time the phone started to ring, my nerves went on edge, anxiety a palpable force coursing through my bloodstream.

"Ellie? I've been so worried."

I had noted the ten missed calls before dialling the number. "I'm sorry."

"I have Étienne in the next room. He keeps asking if you've called and all I keep saying is that you're probably busy. I told him you'd call after supper, but time's been passing, and you haven't been calling, and I was just about ready to send Bernard after you—"

"Please don't do that, Sally," I interjected through her tirade. "I'm fine."

"I don't believe you. This morning—"

"I was just frazzled. I hit a snag, but things are okay now. I think everything will be solved by tonight."

"And you'll be home soon?"

"Soon as I can." There. That was the second time.

Rosalie's perception of bullshit was a little more astute than Catherine's—it helped that she knew what I was actually doing in Quebec City.

"What's happening tonight?"

"I'd rather not talk about it."

"Because it means telling more lies." Rosalie's voice lacked the anger she had every right to use against me. Instead, it was soft with helplessness. "I'm worried about you, Ellie. Do you plan on coming home?"

I should have lied again, but at that moment I was overwhelmed by the need to let someone know something closer to the truth. "I really want to say yes to that."

"Come home, Ellie. Now. We'll figure something else out."

"I'll come when this is done." I used my best reassuring voice to make the promise to her, hopeful she would forget my slip.

"If I wasn't afraid of the answer you'd give me, I'd make you promise me that you'll come home alive and in one piece."

"Well, I definitely can't promise the one piece part." Intended as a joke, my delivery failed to properly express it. Rosalie never would have been entertained by it anyway. "Before I forget," I added to cut through the weighty tension that now held us, "Thank you for always being there for me. And for Étienne."

"I don't like the sound of that. I'm not saying goodbye, Ellie."

"Neither am I."

I heard a small voice in the background. "Etienne wants to talk to you."

"I love you, Rosalie."

"I love you too, Eléonore."

Saying goodbye to my best friend broke my heart.

Saying goodbye to Étienne shattered it.

"I'm so sorry, Maman! I don't know why I spoke to you like I did this morning. I miss you. I just want you back. Are you coming home soon?"

"As soon as I can." My voice cracked the third time saying the lie.

137

"Tomorrow?"

"If I can, I'll be there… I just want you to know how much I love you, mon p'tit prince."

"Come home, Maman."

"Étienne…"

"Please come home."

I could hear the tears in his eyes, though I could not see them. And I could feel myself slowly being torn apart inside. Dying tonight couldn't be worse than this moment when I knew that I would never hear my son's voice again.

"Please, mon p'tit prince. Don't make this… I want to be with you. I wish I could be with you right now."

"Can you be?"

"I wish…"

"Maman, please…"

"Étienne, I can't!" I raised my voice. I hated myself for it, but I had to stop his tirade.

The silence that echoed on the other side was louder than his pleas. It crashed against my ear. "Remember what I told you your first day?"

"That we would have Pouding Chômeur?"

I laughed, but it didn't hit my heart the way Catherine's joke had. "Before that."

"You told me to be brave."

"Do you think you could be brave for me again?"

"Can you promise that you will come home?"

"Why would you think I wouldn't?"

"Aunt Sally said she thought you wouldn't. I heard her say it to Uncle Bernie."

"I'm coming home when I can." It was just a small lie—a when instead of an if. "Wasn't that the promise? I would come back for you."

"Yes, Maman. But..." He stopped short of pronouncing some condition on it.

Stupidly, I prompted him for it. "But what?"

"The other people didn't promise it."

"What other people, mon p'tit prince?"

"Anyone. Everyone. They didn't promise me that my Maman would come back to me."

I knew my kid was brilliant, but this took me aback.

"Je t'aime, Étienne."

"Je t'aime aussi, Maman. Tellement."

"Right up to the moon and back."

I hung up and stared out the front window for a moment without seeing anything, just picturing Étienne's face in my mind. I closed my eyes, rested my head back, and allowed myself to cry for the last time.

When the last tear had fallen, I revved Marianne and started for Vieux-Quebec, prepared for one last fight.

For my son.

CHAPTER SEVENTEEN

A Climax

Anaïs de Dormant was the first human demon hunter. A noblewoman born in fifteenth century France, she witnessed her tutor conjure a demon one night and began a training of her own into the decimation of the unbound beasts. It was a legacy she passed onto a community of others and her firstborn son. It is that heritage that I honour today.

- January 12th 1995

The trip back to Quebec City was as traffic-laden as expected, but I took the road without grief. Rock ballads filled the empty space around me, and I sang along with them. I focused on the lyrics, and they kept me from reminiscing, from thinking at all.

By the time Marianne reached the dark streets of Vieux-Quebec, my voice was hoarse, but my senses were clear.

On the highway, I made one last call. This one to Raphael. It was one I had debated making and finally decided upon its necessity for two reasons: I couldn't risk him messing up tonight, and I needed an extra security measure in case things got messed up anyway.

"Léo. I've been so—"

"I'm sorry about this morning," I spoke hurriedly, forcing myself to sound more anxious than I actually was. "But I need your help. I've done something stupid."

"What is it?" The concern in his voice caught me off-guard.

"I..." I cleared my throat. "Étienne's in trouble. Edmond... He's going to take him. He might already have him. Raphael..."

"Where are you?"

"I'm heading to Montreal, but I don't know... Please, Raph, I need your help. Can you get to Montreal? Can you make sure Étienne is safe? I'll meet you there."

"I'm on my way. Everything's going to be okay, Léo. Promise."

"Thank you." I hung up and took a deep breath. Lying to him had been harder than I had anticipated, but I felt relieved in that moment. Étienne would be safer this way.

I was ready. For whatever came next.

Up the mountain, I drove to the Plains of Abraham. I expected a struggle once I arrived, but the grounds were devoid of life. Any of the guards that would have stood in my way lay on the field, unconscious. They were alive, though. That was a good thing.

It meant that Edmond was already waiting for me, somewhere in the dark. I tingled with excitement. It was that death rush again, knowing that these might be my final moments, knowing that this could be it. Dread crept with the knowing this time because it was not only my life that dangled on the line.

I thought of calling Rosalie again, to say goodnight to Étienne, to hear his voice one more time, but even the thought threatened to break my resolve. I had prepared an email earlier that day to send automatically tomorrow at noon explaining the circumstances to Rosalie. I had attached a letter with it, one for Étienne to read when he was old enough to understand that this was a sacrifice. This was my way of showing love to him. Not that you could ever determine an age when someone could ever really

141

understand that dying was for the best. Ten years on, I still struggled with the concept of my father's passing.

Though I came, a willing sacrifice, I had prepared for war.

Éponine and Trudeau were with me, my faithful companions. I would feel naked without them by my side. They weren't the only weapons I carried on my person. There were three hunting knives shoved into the nifty pouches sewn into my jeans. But the weapon that I would have to rely on was the one that had failed my father that night. Words.

The moon was high in the sky, its white light bright. A late summer evening, the air was warm, but not too hot. I was glad I had chosen to wear a loose shirt over my camisole. I'd be perspiring in anything thicker. Not that it really mattered what I was wearing. Some people died naked as they were born. Some died in Victoria Secret lingerie. Some died in Prada. I was wearing something that I had picked up at one of those mall outlets.

Not that it mattered.

The Citadelle was one of those historic places that most people in Quebec knew about but couldn't name. The largest British fortress in North America, it was now a tourist spot that people frequented to discover the military history of the city. Built in the 1800s after the War of 1812, it was still actively used as a garrison. It was an impressive architectural structure, nearly resembling a pentagram from the air.

I had been here once with my father. We had taken the whole tour the year I had turned thirteen. He had wanted to show me that history was full of conflict to explain why it was so in our present. It was then that he had told me more about our family legacy and the demonic powers that had raged on both sides. Stories too long to share now.

Edmond was waiting for me somewhere within. I couldn't know where for sure, but I made my way to the Dalhousie Gate. Going in through the main entrance made me feel less guilty about sneaking into the place.

The guard that had been stationed there lay asleep on the ground beside the archway. The gate that should have been closed wasn't. I started down the passageway that led into the heart of the Citadelle. There was a dim light shining, but otherwise, it was dark and difficult to perceive anything lingering in the shadows.

Entering the fortifications, I felt a rush, not unlike the one I had felt as a younger child. It might be incredible to believe, but I could still remember that feeling. It was like I was trespassing on a history that was at once mine and someone else's. I could almost imagine that the end of this passage would lead me into a different time, into the early nineteenth century.

I emerged into the night sky again, surrounded now by the mighty stone walls that had been constructed centuries ago to dissuade invaders. To my immediate left, a cross stood, erected in memory of the victory of Vimy Ridge. "Victory for Canadians. Bad day for the Germans." That's what my dad had said. "The triumphant used to write history. They picked their truths, then blended in some exaggerations and straight out lies. School taught that the Germans started World War I. But you know who really started it?"

It hadn't been a rhetorical question. I shook my head.

"No one else does either. Question everything."

Our battle was one of brawn, but my dad had never diminished the strength of brain.

Edmond wasn't in sight, not as far as I could see. He was toying with me. The Citadelle was vast, a maze in some ways. There were no dead ends or fatal traps to confound the normal tourist, but there was every chance of me having to face such obstacles if I didn't consider carefully where he might be lurking.

I did a quick search through my mind, trying to recall what possible locations there were.

The Cap Diamant Redoubt was the oldest military structure in Quebec.

The Regimental Chapel held obvious religious connotations.

The Prince of Wales Bastion…

I knew with a certainty that most people would probably call intuition that I would find him there. Royally named and Quebec City's highest natural point, it also bore a great 12-tonne cannon. A place to feel empowered.

Energy flared within me, and I took the path at a jog. It took me between the regimental housing and the fortified wall. The night was eerily quiet; I took note of it as I went. I had expected some sort of drumming noise to match the pounding in my heart. In the silence, the anxiety I wished I could staunch built the closer I came to the spot.

The path led me to the Royal 22nd Regimental Museum that marked the entrance to the Bastion. I remembered this place too. What had once been a powder magazine had been transformed into a permanent exhibition. My father had told me something when we had reached it. I couldn't remember his exact words, but the gist of them was: "People build museums to remember the false histories and cement them into visuals that people can look at, ooh and ahh at, and feel affected by until ten minutes later when they're stuffing bags with merchandise at the gift shop. People don't know how to live history anymore."

I never had realized how cynical my dad was. But I understood his perspective now. Perhaps, it was inevitable that those of us who saw the real danger of the world also knew that people were good at lying, and hiding and avoiding truths they didn't want to see.

The last stretch to the Bastion required an uphill ascent, though not a very steep one. Pursuing the incline, I couldn't help but think that the higher I went, the less of a distance there would be for my soul to travel—if my soul was bound that way. If that way was even a thing to expect. Heaven that is.

I saw Edmond. He stood beside the cannon, his back to me, gazing out over the St. Lawrence River like some sentry of old keeping watch for enemies.

He was staring in the wrong direction if he was waiting for a fight. His dress was more appropriate, though.

He had shed his casual wear of the morning for something that I could recognise as a classic Elder robe. It was a scarlet colour, but it looked garnet in the darkness of the night. Emblazoned on the back was a gold Fleur de Lys that seemed to shine with its own light.

I unsheathed Éponine. If I was stealthy enough, I could take him unawares. Maybe even kill him.

It was worth a try.

With a deep breath, I leaped forward on the toe of my shoes to keep me aloft and on pace. Éponine was brandished, aimed at the left side of his back. She would pierce him in a fluid motion.

The moonlight shifted. Edmond's form flickered.

145

Too late I realized that he was not standing in front of me at all.

Éponine shot through the illusion. I whipped around as the holographic image dissolved.

Edmond's laugh boomed out in time with his applause. He stood wearing the same red cloak. Beneath it, he wore black slacks and a black shirt.

"Oh, how wonderful! You do have spirit, then. Yes, well done! Well done, indeed, you marvellous creature you!"

If there was a compliment to be taken from that, I did not hear it. All I could detect was belittlement; all I felt was irritation. He was making a fool of me.

"I'm here."

"Yes, I see that. I am frankly impressed that you knew where to come."

"You're an easy man to read."

"Do you really think so?" He approached me, hands at his side.

My grip on Éponine tightened.

"If you hope to kill me with that, you will find it to be a foolish whim."

"What is it that you expect me to do? Die quietly?"

"If I want you to die, it must be loud and painful."

It was the nonchalant way he said it that set my heart racing at a furious pace. "If your plan is to kill me, I'm not going to make it easy."

"Not even if Étienne's life depended on it?"

My arm lowered a little. I had come; that had been the request. I had expected death; I hadn't anticipated that he would want to make a game of it. "Why would it matter to you, either way? Painful or quick? Loud or silent? Why do you want me dead?"

"I do not want you dead."

"Then what do you want from me?"

"Your death."

It was fancy wordplay, but I had no time to appreciate what meaning he might be going for.

Edmond raised his hand, and a jet of gold light flew at me.

I raised Éponine in defence and the blade sliced through the stream. One strand sailed past me, but the second collided with my arm.

The pain that shot through me was unbearable.

In defence, my mind fell into the blackness of its unconscious.

When I came to, I was lying face down on the grass, Éponine smoking a little ways from me. It was miraculous that she was in one piece at all.

"An impressive weapon."

In that time, Edmond had crossed the distance to my side. Still dazed, I could only watch helplessly as he snatched Éponine from the ground and turned her over in his hand. His eyes scrutinised her with a combination of curiosity and wonder. "Wherever did you find it?"

I heaved myself off the floor, my breathing shallow. The pain had passed, but the threat of it was still prevalent.

"Can't remember."

He slid the blade across his palm. Blood pooled from the shallow wound. "Can't you?" His fascination was deeply set.

My hand fumbled for Trudeau, and I drew him out, the blade cutting through the air.

It froze in place, met by some invisible barrier.

"You really don't know me well at all," Edmond mused. His gaze had never faltered from his bleeding palm. I watched as the skin patched up on its own. He carelessly wiped away the blood on his shirt.

Finally, his eyes lifted. They appraised me with intrigue, gazing beyond my own eyes, to somewhere that was hidden within the depth of me.

Could he see the shape of my hatred, the burning ire that tore through me, interfering with my breaths? Could he see the fear I held for my son's wellbeing? Could he see the darkness that was there?

"Put down your weapon, Eléonore."

I could not ignore the power of his persuasive request. My fist uncurled, releasing the hilt. Trudeau fell to the ground.

"Now, kneel."

This time, I resisted the lure of his voice. My knees quivered with the need to obey, but I would not be commanded like some puppet. The pain of remaining standing wasn't nearly as bad as the attack that had run through me before. The more I fought it, the easier it became, my mind accepting its own strength. Soon, even my knees discovered that they did not have to fall to the ground and straightened out. My body grew taller, my posture composed to prove that I would not be played with.

"A firm willpower. It is not often that I encounter one such as yourself. You continue to delight me, Mademoiselle Dormant." With a fluid move, Edmond directed Éponine at my chest, the tip of her wavering over my breastbone. "I cannot believe it took me so long to find you."

"You've gone through a lot of trouble just to kill me." I could hear the weariness in my own voice. I was tired of standing still. It wouldn't be long now before he finally did me in, and if I didn't take him with me, I couldn't guarantee that Étienne would be left alone. "Why don't you just get it over with?"

His eyes shone with amusement. The smile that took his lips was one that contained a secret. "But I have already said I do not want you dead."

"You want my death. You can't tell me that you think there's a difference between the two."

"And yet there is."

He lowered Éponine, dragging the blade through the grass. At that moment, I jumped towards him. Whatever protection he held around him, prevented me from coming within a foot of him.

His laughter was sharp, but it faded when I wielded my next greatest weapon against him: my words.

"*Bonitas ortum. Malum equitat. Vires eius. Mutare aestus.*"

The earth trembled in response. What obstructed my hand shivered.

Edmond's eyes were bright with awe, caught off-guard, so I pressed on.

"*Audite preces. Verba faciam. Conteram murum. Concutite clypeus.*"

By some grace, it did.

My hands moved past the obstruction that had stopped them before and grasped the edges of Edmond's robes. In pure self-defence 101, my knee went up and connected with his crotch.

Edmond doubled over, and my knee rose again, this time connecting with his face. With satisfaction, I heard the crack of his nose breaking. Even an Elder could be taken down by the basics when he was in shock.

With a loud grunt, I whirled him around and flung his body to the ground.

Éponine fell from his grasp. I retrieved her and charged.

Edmond rolled over to avoid Éponine's stabbing motion. Adrenaline kept my movements fast, and I whirled around to strike at him again.

A jet of gold shot towards me. Éponine fell to deflect it. This time it rebounded towards the sorcerer.

He scrambled out of the way. All his self-assured cockiness was gone. Blood smeared his face, his expression contorted with surprised rage.

For the first time, I let myself believe that there was a chance of me getting out of this alive.

Edmond had managed to get to his feet, but there was an unsteadiness in him that I took full advantage of. Even as he found his grounding, I launched at him again. Éponine cleaved through the air towards his stomach. I wanted him to suffer some pain before I ended this.

A sword of his own shimmered into existence. It fell to block my blow and forced me to leap back. His blade shone gold in the moonlight, its scarlet hilt a perfect match to his robe.

"How dare you use words," he hissed at me.

With each slashing arc that he made with his blade, blasts of power radiated, surges that caused me to falter, again and again, forcing me into a defencive stance. Éponine proved her ability to withstand the magic that Edmond possessed, deflecting both his physical blade and ethereal attack. She alone kept me from falling to him. It was my own failing that eventually led me to the edge of the Bastion and the long fall that waited beyond it.

He retreated a step as he realized the same, the blade evaporating from his hand. His chest heaved from the effort of our battle, but his face no longer showed his contempt. Rather, he grinned with a youthful exuberance. "It has been many centuries since I have had the pleasure of such a sparring. I thank you for the diverting sport. But we really must return to business."

I stepped towards him, but he dematerialised, appearing again a bit further down the hill. A snap of his fingers and three looming figures appeared before him.

His demons towered taller over him, large and imposing beings. These were not crudely summoned servants, but the truer terrors that existed in nightmares. They were all the same ebony colour, nearly camouflaged in the darkness that surrounded them. Tails wound from their backsides, thick and jutting with spikes. Their eyes were redder and blood-hungry, their mouths gaping to reveal the sharpest yellow fangs. Each bore a single horn on their head that curved down from their forehead and protruded almost exactly where their nose would have been.

My stance dropped with my heart as they charged me. Was this what he had meant by my death? Were these demons the final blow? Was my soul about to be claimed by evil? Had that been his intention?

For Étienne, I could not simply relinquish to them.

151

I darted forward to meet them, and the distance between us closed.

A blinding orange light filled the area, burning bright and hot like the sun. I shielded my eyes, but my ears remained unblocked. The shrieks of the demons were shrill and piercing, sounds I'd rather not have heard, that I would never be able to forget.

The light faded, and I risked opening my eyes.

A red and gold demon stood before me, as majestic as the others were moribund. They were melting, whatever remained of their forms dripping to the ground in oozing black puddles that burned the grass beneath them.

Edmond's seething voice carved through the air. "I warned you to come alone. For your son's sake."

"I did," I protested, circling the demon that had saved me.

"Then explain this."

I wanted an explanation too. The demon turned towards me, the colour of its scales shimmering. It looked more like a dragon than anything, its body lizard-like and winged. I had seen an image of such a creature before, in a book my father had kept on demons. It was, I realized, one of the Ruinangelus, the first of demons. In the next moment, a name came to my mind.

"Kerryn?"

One gold-flecked amber eye winked at me. The demon trembled, her light fading as she shrunk down, resuming the shape of the teenager I could recognise.

"You're welcome," she said, and then vanished from sight.

"What treachery is this now?"

Edmond's voice drew my gaze towards him. A flicker of movement behind him distracted me from the irritation he exuded.

Raphael stalked towards us, lithe and agile, nearly invisible in the shadow of nights.

I turned my eyes from him, but too late. My staring had betrayed the aid that came, uncalled for and unwanted as it was.

Edmond whirled, and a gold stream flew towards Raphael.

Raphael jerked right, dodging the blast, and then shot forth his own turquoise stream.

Edmond evaded the attack. The light continued on course towards me.

I jumped out of the way and nearly tripped over my feet.

"What are you doing here? Go away!" I shouted at him.

"Yes, listen to the lady. She does not wish to have your assistance. Leave now, and I will let you live."

"She does not command me, and neither do you," Raphael asserted. His body twisted and then came around again, sweeping a gust of wind that came too quick for Edmond to avoid. It knocked him to the ground.

Raphael moved towards me. "You lied to me."

"I was trying to protect Étienne."

"He's safe. But you're not. Leave now, and I'll take care of him."

"The deal was I get to kill him," I argued, my eyes darting towards Edmond's stirring form.

Raphael saw it too. His hands reached up and ensnared the air. He threw it, but Edmond was on his feet and ready this time. He caught the gust of wind and hurled it towards me.

I raised Éponine, and the current of wind barrelled past me without harming me. I stumbled, the force of nature difficult to stand against.

I didn't expect it to whip around again.

Raphael did.

Arms shoved me from the path of the returning wind. It captured Raphael instead, dragging him to Edmond and raising him high in the air.

"You are not supposed to be here, Raphael. The safety of her son depended on that."

"I didn't ask him to come!" I hurried towards them but came to a halt when Edmond looked towards me, his hand raising. There was no power in it, but it stilled me nonetheless.

"And yet here he is." Edmond's voice oozed maliciousness. "And I think someone must suffer for it."

"Not my son."

"I agree."

The wind spun faster and faster, ensnaring Raphael entirely.

The breath caught in my throat at as I felt Raphael gasping for air. "Stop!"

I dashed forward, Éponine prepared to deal a death blow.

Edmond raised a hand, and a projection of power propelled me back.

I crashed against the ground and pain shot up my injured shoulder. It was nothing compared to the ache I felt as Raphael suffocated above me. I could not live with another man being doomed to death because of me.

Rising to my feet, I propelled myself towards Edmond. Three more times I made an attempt. Each time I did, he flung me back, every repulsion revealing more fury. The last time I nearly rolled off the cliff and scrambled to stop my body from completing the plunge.

Edmond flung his hands down. As he did, Raphael's body crashed into the ground with enough force to cause a crater to form beneath him.

He was still alive. Though he showed no movement, I knew it with the same certainty that I knew I was living. His body was still and broken, but I could sense his heartbeat.

Edmond summoned his sword from the air as he had before. He stared into my eyes. "I will take his life and then I will take your son's."

Without turning away from me, he lifted his blade. I saw in his eyes the determination to kill, to exact punishment.

Where helplessness should have burned within me, a deeper ferocity coursed through my veins. It was all of me, this strong emotion. The desire to protect my son, to protect his father, would not let me sit still. And in the face of the impossibility of acting, my mind created a new alternative.

I felt the power of my urge build within me until it sparked at my fingertips. The darkness of my thirst for death was frightening, palpable, and overwhelming. It clouded my judgement until it was all I knew. There was no room for my reasoning powers. It was pure instinct that guided me, reaching into a place that I had not known existed and summoning from it a magic that was all my own.

A cloud of darkness rose up from my hands, rising above my head.

Edmond watched it all. I saw him through the fog that blocked my vision. In his face, I saw such pleasure, admiration, and veneration. "Yes," he shouted, though I heard it only as a whisper. "Give me your death."

And so I did, not because he asked for it, but because it was my wish.

The cloud I had created shot forward and grasped Edmond in a suffocating grip. He laughed as it ensnared him. It broke through his body and tore his spirit from him. The darkness devoured it and his life and then blew away with a sweeping gust of air.

Edmond's body collapsed to the ground and, as it came into contact with it, dissolved into Autumn coloured leaves.

CHAPTER EIGHTEEN

A Return

The Ruinangelus is believed to be more than demon. With Lucifer, they fell from the heavens and created Daemoniar. They have never been summoned, nor are they known to cross over. The sole transcribed sighting describes them as dragonesque figures. Most hunters I have met believe that they are only a myth.

- September 1st 1994

I didn't have time to worry about what had just happened, not while Raphael's life was fading from him.

I ran to his side and fell onto the ground beside him. Suddenly it wasn't Raphael lying broken in front of me. It was my father.

I stumbled back, but then I saw that it really was Raphael. My mind was playing tricks with me.

His eyes were shut, his mouth pursed in pain. His breathing was belaboured and barely noticeable. I didn't know how many bones in his body were broken or how much internal damage he had sustained. But he could heal himself. He just needed to wake up.

"Raphael!"

I shook him hard.

He grunted, his eyes fluttering open.

"Léo…" He hacked my name.

"Heal yourself, damn you! C'mon, Raph!" I shook him again as his eyes shut. Each time he fell towards an unconscious state he drew closer to a final rest that he could not come back from. Each time he opened his eyes, I could feel the life that was still there. "Don't give up on me."

"Edmond…?"

"He's fallen leaves now."

"Is that… supp… supposed to… be poetic…"

"It's just a matter of fact. Now, heal yourself."

His beautiful eyes were dimmer than I'd ever seen them before. "Can't," he whispered. "Too much… damage…"

He wasn't lying, but I wouldn't accept his word. "So you're going to prove me right on the solo thing?"

"Unfortunately…"

"You're supposed to say no."

Raphael didn't give an answer. His eyes had closed again, his chest nearly still.

"C'mon Raph!" I gave him another shake. "Use me."

His eyelids came halfway up his eyes. "Léo, no…"

He was too weak to deny me this request; I willed him to take some of my life, to use my strength to heal himself. There was a swell of power within me, such as I had felt before decimating Edmond. This time, the force was guided by love, not hate.

My energy left me, slipping into Raphael. Through blurred vision, I watched as his wounds slowly mended and, his body became whole once more.

When it was done, I stumbled back, overcome by weariness.

Raphael sat up, reaching for me, his expression one of bewilderment and concern.

"What a crazy night, huh?" The remaining strength I possessed fled me, and I keeled over. Blissfully, I fell into the recess of my own unconscious where no thoughts existed.

⚜ ⚜ ⚜ ⚜ ⚜ ⚜

I awoke, certain that I had been dreaming of a battle upon the Prince of Wales Bastion, and discovering that I suddenly possessed some sort of magical prowess.

The delusion lasted as long as it took for me to take another breath.

"You didn't tell me you were an *Inionaofa*."

Kerryn sat at the edge of my bed. We were in Raphael's guest bedroom, the first light of dawn brightening the room.

I blinked at her, rubbing my eyes. She smirked at my bleariness. Soon it became clear that she wasn't just an illusion.

"You didn't tell me you were a Ruinangelus."

She shrugged. "It wasn't anything you had to know. What's your story?"

"What in hellfire is an *Inionaofa*?"

"Ah, you don't know."

"But you do. So spill."

"It's not my place to say." She stood up, twirling a strand of hair. "Raph doesn't know I'm here, by the way. Better he doesn't know I was."

"Why?"

"Because I'm not his anymore, and I don't want him to think I'm interested. And because, if you do, I'll make your life a living hell."

"You might be too late for that."

Kerryn giggled. "I want us to be allies, Eléonore. Would you like that?"

159

"Not sure. What do you want in return?"

"Your help."

"With?"

"We can't play the game of trust if I spell everything out for you."

"What do I get in return?"

"Well, now that I'm unbound, I can guarantee that no one touches your son. Consider that bounty as good as gone."

That was an offer I couldn't refuse. "Then, let's play the trust game."

"Superb!" She winked at me, then twirled. Her gold skirt swirled around her, and she vanished into it.

My shoulder ached as I rose from the bed. A bit of Sinéad's concoction would help with that. My head pounded away too. Two painkillers wouldn't hurt either.

The potion went down easily, the effect immediate. Out of the pill bottle tumbled my faithful friends. They landed in my open palm, and I stuffed them into my mouth before realising I didn't have water to help swallow them down.

I made for the kitchen and found that Raphael actually was awake and brewing a pot of coffee.

He turned as he heard me enter. "Bon matin."

I nodded and went into the fridge for a bottle of water. With a swig, I downed half its contents and the two pills. Gagging a little, I finally gave him my reply. "Is that what we say after what happened?"

"The alternative is what in the damnation of all things good and holy happened last night?"

"I can stick with a good morning for now."

I sat down at the table and waited until he brought me over a mug of coffee. We sat opposite each other, silent, sipping the dark liquid. The heat it brought helped to diminish the cold feeling in my gut. My mind slipped into consideration of what had happened the night before. Of the magic that I had wielded, that I had never known I could wield before.

I could see Edmond's face and the pleasure in it as my power had destroyed him. He had wanted *my death.* Is that what he had meant?

It was too much for me to dwell on.

"I guess you'll be leaving today," Raphael said, allowing me a distraction from the thoughts I feared.

"Soon as I'm done with this cup of coffee." I had meant it as a joke, but we both understood it to be truth.

"Étienne will be glad to see you again."

I nodded and then remembered the email I had prepared. "Merde." I pulled out my phone.

"What's wrong?"

"Nothing." I cancelled the scheduled message, saving it into drafts. Just in case.

"That's not entirely true, though."

"No." We stared at each other. "But I don't want to talk about it."

"You saved my life."

"Don't ask me how,'cause I have no idea in hell."

He reached for my hand. "I still want to thank you. I'd be dead if it weren't for you."

I sighed as his hand came into contact with mine. There was no spark, but a comfortable warmth. A companionable touch. "I think that goes two ways."

"I won't ask you about last night," he said after a time, retracting his hand. "But I would ask you something else. If I may."

"What?" I was more suspicious of what his question would be than curious. There was still a lot of mystery between us, and after my bizarre encounter with Kerryn this morning, I wasn't sure what to expect from him.

"Étienne. Léo, I know what we said, but couldn't I—?"

"No," I declared firmly, shaking my head. "No, you can't." Perhaps it was mean of me, but I couldn't give him permission to meet with Étienne. It wasn't because I didn't trust him, but I wasn't ready for Étienne to discover that I had spewed half-truths about his father. Last night I had caved because it seemed like the best and only option available to me. In the light of day, things looked different.

Raphael sank back, not fighting me. It was the look of genuine dismay on his face that convinced me to add, "Not right now."

He sat up a little straighter, eyes alight with hope. "But one day?"

"Maybe."

"I'll take it."

I drained the last of the coffee in my mug.

"Guess you'll be leaving now?"

I glanced towards the pot. There was enough left to cover us each at least once more. "I wouldn't say no to a refill."

"Sounds good to me."

We didn't talk much after that, drinking in an agreed silence, just glad to be alive and, for the moment, friends again. As long as we didn't talk about what had happened, we could be perfectly amicable.

When the last of the coffee had been drained, I finally admitted that it was time to be off. The caffeine had only helped to enhance my eagerness to return home to Étienne. Raphael carried my bag, though I had done my best to convince him it wasn't necessary.

"You drive safe now."

"One-oh-five, stay alive."

"And if you're ever in town…"

"I'm sure I could find my way here again."

He hugged me before I could escape into Marianne's front seat. "Be careful, Léo. I don't know what's going on, and I know you don't really want to talk about it with me, but you need to figure it out. Try Sinéad. She should know something."

I had already drawn the same conclusion. Interrogating her about what had transpired was one of my top priorities going forward. Étienne came first, though. That was at the top of my list of things to do once I made my way to Montreal. Tomorrow I would seek out Sinéad, but today was for Étienne…

"Oh, merde!"

"What is it?"

I waved away his concern. "I promised Étienne I'd bring him back a gift."

Raphael's features relaxed. Lucky for him he could consider it a minor problem; I didn't have that luxury. I needed something special to bring back to Étienne. The search for such a treasure was bound to be more difficult than finding Edmond.

"I might have something."

I raised a quizzical brow. "It needs to be heartfelt."

163

"I have something," he repeated and ran back into his house before I could argue against it.

I waited, part of me hoping that Raphael really did have something wonderful up his sleeve. It would make everything so much easier for me.

He returned, clutching a hardcover book in his hand. He offered it to me. "I've had this for a while."

I took one look at the title and had to swallow down a gasp of surprise. It was a copy of *Le Petite Prince,* a first edition.

"I heard you talking to Étienne... You called him... I thought."

"It's perfect," I told him once I had found my voice. I embraced him again, meaning the gesture of gratitude. It bothered me a bit to have to accept his generosity, but I was glad to save myself the time otherwise. And it really was a wonderful gift.

"Glad to be of help," Raphael said and released me with a wink. "And I really do want to help you, Léo."

"I know, Raph." Before I could stop myself, I added, "And if I need, I'll ask."

I didn't know what possessed me to say it to him. I wasn't even sure that I was convinced that I would extend the same to him, but it felt right to say it at that moment. And there was a part of me that was glad to think that if push came to shove, I would have an ally to turn to. Maybe one thing this trip had taught me was that hunting solo wasn't the best way to go about things. It had felt good to have someone to fight with again. Not that I would admit it to Raphael.

The ride back to Montreal seemed long and yet short at the same time. The anticipation and impatience I felt to be reunited with my son made it feel like I was moving in slow motion, while the knowledge that I was going home made each passed landmark feel like it hadn't taken so long to get there. For once, I was moving in real time.

It was nearly four o'clock when I got into the city, manoeuvring through traffic. To see the familiar buildings of home brought joy to my heart.

More than that, it brought an eagerness to return to the way that life had been.

I forgot for a moment that it was, in all likelihood, impossible that I would ever recapture the status quo again.

I didn't bother to call before I arrived, pulling up in front of Bernard's home and leaping out of Marianne without pausing to consider who might see me. Kerryn had promised we would be left alone and I was willing to play the trust game with her.

The door bell rang, and seconds later Rosalie appeared at the door.

She shrieked loudly and enveloped me in her arms.

"Étienne!" she shouted. "Come here!"

I could hear his feet pounding against the floor then saw his flushed face push between Rosalie's frame and mine.

"Maman!" He shouted with a glee that resonated with the exploding contentment that constricted my chest.

I embraced him, kneeling on the floor so that we were as close as possible. His head burrowed into my shoulder and mine is his.

"I came home, mon p'tit prince. And I brought you a gift." I passed him the first edition.

He stared at it, then back up at me. "I'm just glad you're back." He embraced me again, and I clutched him close.

We had survived this ordeal, and I was content to relax in the knowledge of it. I knew that there were still a lot of demons to kill, both physical and surreal kinds, but Étienne was safe, and I was home. We were together again. I would cherish my time with him, devote myself to him for as long as I could.

At least, until the next hellhole of trouble found its way to me.

APPENDIX

(The extra features at the end of this book, not the anatomical part)

dramatis personae

Eléonore Dormant:

Me. Single Mother. Demon Hunter by night. Librarian by day. I reckon that's enough for you to go on.

Étienne Dormant:

Named after my father.
My son, mon p'tit prince. The centre of my universe.
Touch him and you die.

Rosalie Lavigne:

(affectionately, Sally)
The Thelma to my Louise. The Elinor to my Marianne. The Mother Hen to my fledgling chick.

Sinéad Quirke:

African and Irish heritage. My surrogate mother. My personal wise woman. The closest thing I know to a living goddess.

Catherine Fontaine:

The world's best boss. Literally. Big, bubbly personality. Big, generous heart.
Niggle: insists on setting me up with one of her sons.

Bernard Sauveur:

Surgeon at MUHC. I call on his medical skills and discretion when necessary.
Engaged to my Sally. Unworthy of her love.

Raphael Pelletier:

Étienne's father.
A terrible mistake. The man, not my son. Damn strange how that happens.

A Hierarchy of Sorcery

ANCIENT

Over 500. Most powerful class.
Born with sorcery in their blood.
Immortal. Can warp space, heal
the injured, raise the dead.

ELDER

200–500 years old. Magic born or
learned. Not all become
Ancients. Can travel through
space and heal the injured.

NOVICE

Train under an Elder. Mostly do
grunge work. Have no
permission to summon demons
or use powerful spells.

A Hierarchy of Demons

RUINANGELUS

Reign over Daemoniar. The religious sorts like to believe they fell from heaven with Lucifer.

ELEMENTAIRE

Control over the five elements. Sorcerers summon their kind the most because their powers blend well together.

TENEBRES

Real nuisances. Cross over on their own. Make trouble however they can, bargaining, casting minor spells, promoting evil.

FAIBLESSE

Powerless losers who serve other demons. No magic to speak of and little to offer besides their ability to lift heavy objects.

November 11th 1990

My life has a new purpose.

Her name is Eléonore.

She is all I have left now. And for Avelynn, I will love her more than anything else in this damned world.

I will raise her to be strong and good. To be wise and open-minded.

To be a demon hunter, and carry on the tradition of our ancestors.

I will train her to be stronger, faster, more ruthless. I will make her tougher so that she can survive.

I will teach her all I know,

I will teach her all I am.

--- --- ---

(an excerpt from my father's journal)

ACKNOWLEDGEMENTS

There are a lot of people to extend thanks to.

First, to my beta readers: Kyle Adams and C.A. Russo. Your suggestions and words of encouragement helped me find the courage to publish my debut.

To my editor, Nicole Dentremont. Your sharp eye was my best friend in this last leg of the race. It saved me the embarrassment of my grammatical shortcomings.

To my cover designer, Ana Grigoriu-Voicu. I cannot believe the beauty that is the cover of this book. You took my vision and gave it life.

To you, my reader. I hope you enjoyed this book, because I wrote it for you. If you are eager for the sequel, then this has been a success. Thank you for giving me a chance.

ABOUT THE AUTHOR

Faith Rivens was born and bred in Montreal, Québec. So it made sense to set her first book in her hometown.

She believes in telling the story in your heart and pursuing those dreams that make you happiest.

This is her first novella, but you can be sure it will not be her last.

Connect with Faith:

Instagram @faith_therivens

Twitter: @faith_therivens

Blog: https://www.aliasfaithrivens.wordpress.com